3 4028 07312 8077
HARRIS COUNTY PUBLIC LIBRARY

YA Brouwe
Brouwer, Sigmund
Oil king courage

WITHDRAWN
$9.95
ocn364989303
01/05/2010

C

D1415039

Sigmund Brouwer

orca sports

ORCA BOOK PUBLISHERS

Copyright © 2009 Sigmund Brouwer

All rights reserved. No part of this publication may be reproduced
or transmitted in any form or by any means, electronic or mechanical,
including photocopying, recording or by any information storage
and retrieval system now known or to be invented, without permission
in writing from the publisher.

Library and Archives Canada Cataloguing in Publication

Brouwer, Sigmund, 1959-
Oil king courage / written by Sigmund Brouwer.

(Orca sports)
ISBN 978-1-55469-197-5

1. Inuit--Juvenile fiction. I. Title. II. Series: Orca sports

PS8553.R68467O34 2009   jC813'.54   C2009-903039-X

Summary: When a pond-hockey tournament takes Gear and his best friend
Reuben to communities across the Arctic, Gear helps his friend solve
a family mystery and connect to his Inuit heritage.

First published in the United States, 2009
Library of Congress Control Number: 2009928873

Orca Book Publishers gratefully acknowledges the support for its publishing
programs provided by the following agencies: the Government of Canada
through the Book Publishing Industry Development Program and the
Canada Council for the Arts, and the Province of British Columbia through
the BC Arts Council and the Book Publishing Tax Credit.

Cover design by Teresa Bubela
Cover photography by Getty Images
Author photo by Bill Bilsley

Orca Book Publishers   Orca Book Publishers
PO Box 5626, Stn. B   PO Box 468
Victoria, BC Canada   Custer, WA USA
V8R 6S4   98240-0468

www.orcabook.com
Printed and bound in Canada.
Printed on 100% PCW recycled paper.

12 11 10 09 • 4 3 2 1

This book is dedicated to the real Gear.
You know who you are. You are a true friend
to the Arctic and the people who live there.
I'm grateful for our friendship.

chapter one

If a guy could choose how he was going to die, he'd probably hope to be stampeded by cheerleaders, all of them fighting to be the first one to smooch him. He wouldn't want to be running down the ice highway, with a bulldozer chasing him and snot freezing his lips together.

All because of Reuben Reuben and his sister, Lizzie. Whenever she was around, it was hard for me to breathe. That's my

1

excuse, although I have to take some of the blame for what happened.

It started in early September. The Edmonton Oil Kings, a WHL team, were touring the western Arctic for preseason, playing local exhibition games to raise money for charity and to promote a literacy program for kids. One of their last games was here in Inuvik, where Reuben and Lizzie and I went to high school at Samuel Hearne Secondary. Reuben and I were both playing for the Inuvik team.

"Ready for the game?" I said to Reuben during the pregame skate.

"Sure, Gear."

My real name is Gary Itskut. I moved to Inuvik from Norway when I was seven and my dad was still part of the family. He left. My mom and I stayed. I'm called Gear because people say I pronounce my own name like that. They also call me Gear because I like taking things apart to see how they work. If Reuben was one of the best hockey players around, I was

one of the best geeks. It seemed I understood engineering stuff as naturally as
he understood how to flick a wrist shot
into a corner of the net. When I took
something apart and put it back together,
chances were it would work even better
than before.

"Other things on your mind?" I asked.
He seemed distracted. "Like the booger
hanging from your nose?"

Reuben wiped his nose without even
getting upset that I was messing with him.
Not good.

"What's up?" I said.

"I don't want to go to school anymore."

"Huh? We promised each other."
Reuben was my best friend. I talked to
him all the time about going south after
high school. We'd go to college or university together. I was working hard to get a
scholarship, and I was helping him work
for one too.

"I know I promised," Reuben said, "but
some days I think Grandma Nellie is right.

We can't forget how to live the traditional ways."

"We've been through this," I said. "The North is changing. You need to—"

The ref blew his whistle, and I didn't have a chance to finish. Besides, I had other things to worry about in the near future. Like survival on the ice. After all, I was a geek. Not a hockey player.

In the face-off circle, I faced a center named Godzilla.

No, that wasn't his real name. But it should have been.

I'm not short, but I had to crane my head back to look at him. Dark hair curled out from underneath his helmet. He had dark eyes. A big nose. A dark mustache. And a big friendly grin.

"Have fun," he said. It seemed like he meant it. After all, it was only an exhibition game.

Easy for him to say. It was the end of the Oil Kings' exhibition season. They'd been skating most of the summer. It had been months since I'd been on the ice. Plus, I was nervous anyway.

I'm sure he was used to playing in front of crowds much bigger than the one here at Inuvik's arena. For me, and for most of the players on our team, this was as big as it got. Saying the whole town was here to watch wasn't quite true. It was kind of like calling the center Godzilla—a bit of an exaggeration.

On the other hand, if you measured the percentage of the town in the stands, Godzilla had never played in front of a bigger crowd.

Inuvik only has a population of about 3,500. So if there were 500 fans in the stands, that was one person out of every seven. Fourteen point three percent. For Godzilla, if Edmonton's population is a million, that would be like skating in front of a crowd of about 143,000 people.

I was unable to shut my brain off. I thought of something else. We lived so far north and it was so remote that if you drew a 180-mile circle around Inuvik—the distance from Edmonton to Calgary—that circle might only add another 1,000 people to the total. So 500 out of 4,500 was one out of nine. For convenience in the math, make it one out of ten. Yup. I was playing a crowd that was nearly ten percent of all the people in a 200-mile radius. That's 25,000 square miles.

"Hey." Godzilla's voice interrupted my thoughts. "Have fun," he said again.

That's when I noticed he'd taken his glove off his right hand and was holding his hand out for me to shake.

"Oh," I said. "Sorry. I was kind of lost in thought for a second or two."

The ref had just reached the circle.

I took off my own glove and shook hands with Godzilla.

The ref waited for us to get ready. Then he crouched.

I began to wonder what it would be like to play in front of 143,000 people.

And whether Lizzie would be hanging out with us after the game.

I can't help those kinds of thoughts. They happen all the time. Anytime. Like in front of Godzilla, about a second before the puck dropped. I should have had my head in the game.

Instead I was thinking all those things.

And one other thing.

They didn't know my right winger, Reuben Reuben.

The ref dropped the puck.

chapter two

My hockey was decent, but not WHL level. My best skill—and maybe it was close to WHL level—was that I was good at winning face-offs.

Against Godzilla, as the puck dropped, I got enough weight on my stick to block his stick as he finished sweeping it on his backhand to their left defenseman. Instead of winning the draw clean, Godzilla only managed to get the heel of the blade on the puck. It bounced and wobbled slowly as it headed toward the Oil Kings' blue line.

As the ref dropped the puck, Reuben jumped past his winger. He was half a step into the clear as the puck wobbled toward the Oil Kings' left defenseman, a guy named Slinger.

From my position at center, I saw everything.

Slinger had taken a step toward the puck, but Reuben's quickness caused him to freeze for a second. That left him in a bad position between the blue line and the centerline. Reuben took advantage of it and poked the puck into the open ice between both Oil Kings' defensemen.

Godzilla was trying to get into the play, but I accidentally tugged on his sleeve and held him back for a second. All right, I confess. Maybe it wasn't an accident.

Slinger was too far forward to stop Reuben, but he was committed to lunging forward and couldn't spin fast enough to catch Reuben either.

Their right defenseman had played it safer. He was far enough back to get a good angle on Reuben and was almost close enough to block Reuben's forward progress.

Reuben got the blade of his stick on the puck. Actually, under the puck. He plattered it. For a split second, it rested completely flat on his blade, which was horizontal to the ice. Reuben spun his blade upside down and around again in a tight circular swoop. The puck stayed on his blade, and with a quick move he fired it like a lacrosse shot into the boards just left of the net.

The boom of impact echoed across the ice.

It was a move that obviously confused the second Oil Kings' defenseman, because it froze him too.

Not Reuben. He was skating at full speed, following the puck to get the rebound off the boards. Three strides later, he reached it. Then he pulled it toward his body with his stick and let it past his front foot to the blade of his rear skate.

He kicked the puck forward and caught it on his stick. Faked a shot. Went to his backhand and easily moved past the sprawled goalie.

Wide-open net!

Reuben gently pushed the puck across the goal line, easing it into the back of the net.

In a heartbeat, ten percent of the entire population of 25,000 square miles went nuts!

Reuben gave a quick fist pump as he circled away from the net. But that was it. Showy as the goal was, I knew him well enough not to expect him to raise his stick in the air with both arms high. He wasn't a showboat. His job was to put the puck in the net, so why act like it was a big deal?

As the noise quieted, I drifted alongside Godzilla as we both headed toward center ice for the next face-off.

"Funny," he said, smiling. "For a couple of seconds there, it felt like someone was hanging on to my jersey."

"That was *your* jersey?" I shook my head. "Now everything makes sense. I thought it was mine and that someone was trying to pull it away. That's why I held on so tight."

That made Godzilla laugh. "Not that it would have made a difference. Your buddy beat our defense so bad, I think they accidentally switched jockstraps trying to stop him."

"Yeah," I said. "Notice how the crowd cheered for the way I set it all up off the draw?"

Godzilla shook his head and rolled his eyes. "I thought we were in Inuvik, not fantasy land."

"In my world," I answered, "sometimes I can't tell the difference."

chapter three

Just before the ref dropped the puck again, I backed out of the face-off circle.

"Reuben," I said, "Godzilla here is too strong. There's no way I can get the puck to the right side off the draw. How about switching wings?"

"Godzilla?" Godzilla echoed.

"Think of it as a compliment," I told him. "It's the way I meant it."

But Godzilla's attention had shifted away from me. He was staring at Reuben, who cut across the ice toward the left wing.

In a town as small and remote as ours, pulling together a team meant being less picky than it might have been in other towns. Our own left winger was a big guy named Evan. He was about thirty years old. Unlike Godzilla, who was obviously fast, Evan was big and slow. He had a hard slap shot but needed lots of room and time to fire it. His stickhandling was pathetic. Passes bounced off his stick. When he tried to pass, the puck often ended up under his own skates.

The best part about his game was that he never washed his hockey equipment. When Evan pinned you against the boards with his shoulder, it was like using a skunk for a pillow. So opponents often just let him go into the corner to get the puck without fighting him for it. Most of the time he didn't do anything with the puck anyway.

As Reuben and Evan switched sides, Reuben stopped and offered his stick to Evan. That's why Godzilla wasn't listening to me.

Evan took Reuben's stick. Reuben took Evan's stick.

Evan didn't care that he'd gone from shooting left to shooting right. He was so bad, it really didn't matter.

As for Reuben, his switch from right winger to left winger was complete. He now had a stick curved for someone shooting left.

"Thanks, ref," I said.

"I don't get it," Godzilla said to me as we moved into the face-off circle.

"Be better if Reuben goes to his strong side," I said.

Godzilla was still blinking as he tried to figure this out. He wasn't set when the ref dropped the puck. I was able to pull it back to our left defenseman, who fell as the puck hit his stick.

He looked like easy prey. The Oil Kings' right winger, a short wide guy with the name *Venezia* across his jersey, swooped in for a breakaway. Godzilla jumped into the play too. This left Reuben unguarded in the neutral zone. With me still at center ice too.

But just before the Oil Kings' winger reached the puck, our defenseman flailed in desperation. He managed to nick the puck, and it hopped through Venezia's legs.

Onto Reuben's stick.

With me open.

Reuben slid the puck to me.

I turned like I was going to pass to Evan.

Not likely.

Godzilla had stopped and turned to pursue me.

I flipped the puck back to Reuben.

"All yours," I yelled.

Reuben cut toward the middle of the ice, directly in front of me.

I stayed where I was. I accidentally blocked Godzilla. Okay, it wasn't an accident.

Evan had his winger tied up, so that left Reuben against the two Oil Kings' defensemen. That was the bad news. The good news was that Reuben was in full stride with lots of room.

At least it looked like he was in full stride.

I'm not a good player, but I do try to watch and learn. One thing I knew about good players was that they had more than one speed. Someone like me, always trying his hardest, only has one speed: as fast as I can go.

That makes it too easy for opponents to judge what you are doing.

Reuben had about three different speeds. Right now he was at three-quarters. He stayed on his angle, taking him from our left side across to Slinger, the defense-man on the Oil Kings' left side.

Slinger, I'm sure, was still mad about Reuben's first goal. Slinger saw the angle and moved up to lay a huge body check on Reuben. He didn't know that Reuben could kick it up a notch. And then another notch.

Reuben looks effortless when he plays. In a flash, he was past Slinger, who had braced for impact. He left Slinger looking like a pylon just outside the Oil Kings' blue line.

Reuben was on a half breakaway!

The other defenseman cut across. Just like before.

Reuben didn't mess around. From the top of the face-off circle, stickhandling left-handed instead of right-handed, Reuben snapped a shot that lasered into the top right-hand side of the net.

Once again, chaos in the stands!

And once again, I found myself drifting beside Godzilla toward the face-off circle.

"Like I said," I told Godzilla, "it's better when Reuben shifts to his strong side."

We lost the exhibition game 10–6, but Reuben scored five of our goals. I scored the sixth. And at the end of the game, Godzilla was the first to give him a high five. All the other Oil Kings did the same.

Funny how they ignored me.

chapter four

"What's the problem?" I asked Reuben.

I was sitting on the steps that led to the interior of a Beechcraft 90. The twin turboprop aircraft is one of my favorites to fly. Maybe that gives the wrong impression. I'm not a qualified pilot. Yet. More accurately, among the fleet of MacDelta Air, the Beechcraft 90 is one of my favorites to sit in the copilot seat above the Mackenzie River valley and delta. Eight passenger seats. Pressurized cabin.

Speed: 240 miles per hour. Range: 1,080 miles. Needs only 2,500 feet of runway. A dependable workhorse with personality.

Yup. I loved it. I almost patted the gleaming white paint of the aircraft body.

"Now why would you assume there's a problem?" Reuben said. He frowned. Indignant.

He was interrupting the work I had to do for MacDelta Air to get the plane cleaned up and ready to be chartered the next day. But that was all right. I wasn't in a hurry. I loved being around airplanes. I spent about twenty hours a week in the huge hangars at Mike Zubko Airport, a few miles east of Inuvik. I cleaned planes, loaded planes, did anything that needed to be done. All to be able to continue my flying lessons, so I could fly solo someday.

"Why would I assume you're here with a problem?" I said.

I held up my hand to tick off my fingers one by one.

"First," I said, touching my index finger, "you're pretending to be mad that I would ask. You're not good at pretending. So knock off the tough look. It makes you look goofy."

Finger number two. "If it was anything else, you would have called and saved yourself the trip out here. But you don't like asking me for help, and you've got too much pride to ask over the phone."

Finger three. "It's a problem that's too important for you to wait until I get back into town after work. You hate flying so much that even getting near an airplane makes you itch."

I didn't mention why he was afraid. When he was too young to remember, his parents had died in a small plane crash. His legal guardian was his grandmother, who lived in Aklavik. She had raised Reuben and Lizzie there until they came to high school in Inuvik, where they lived with one of their aunts.

"Does not make me itch," he said.

"So why are you rubbing your neck?"

He glared at me and stopped rubbing. Then he couldn't help himself and began rubbing again.

I touched finger four, my pinkie. "And lastly, whenever you do have problems, you know I'm the best person to help you."

"Well, you're wrong," Reuben said. "I'm not here because of a problem."

"Then it must be more than one problem."

He sighed. "Two problems."

"Hence the reason you come to me. I know so much."

"Hence?" he said.

"Sprinkle words like that in your conversation and chicks think you're cool. It impresses them more when you can score five goals against the Oil Kings, but I've got to work with what I've got."

He sighed again. "Well, that's one of my problems. The Oil Kings' coach came to see me this afternoon before the commercial flight took the team back south."

The Oil Kings flew out on a Boeing 737, part of the Canadian North fleet. Now that is a plane. I started thinking about it. What it would be like to be at the controls of a puppy like that? About three hundred thousand horsepower and—

"Gear! Gear!"

I looked up to see Reuben snapping his fingers in front of my eyes.

"Welcome back," he said. "You have the attention span of a one-year-old."

I coughed. "The Oil Kings' coach called today. They invited you for a tryout."

"You knew about that?"

"Lizzie called me as soon as she heard. I bet everyone in the school knows. But I must be hearing you wrong. You said a chance with the Oil Kings was a problem."

"The coach also said that the Oil Kings place a lot of value on education. He wants a letter from the school to see if I have decent grades. They'd want me to continue school in Edmonton."

Sounded great to me. I'd be down south at the end of the school year too, ready to start college or university in Edmonton.

"Here's my advice," I said. "Tell the coach you'll continue to score five goals a game."

"I did. He said school mattered. A lot."

My turn to sigh. Reuben wasn't as motivated by school as I was. "Yes, that's definitely a problem. Unless you're willing to start working on it."

"I'm not the gearhead who reads something once and remembers it forever."

"You can get great grades if you want to."

"I want to," Reuben said, "but there's a bigger problem. I need to get to Aklavik and back before tomorrow's commercial flight to Edmonton."

There were no roads across the delta. In the summer, you went by boat. In the winter, by ice highway. Unless you wanted to fly.

"You willing to go in this?" I pointed at the plane beside me. "We can charter this tomorrow. I've built up some credit."

"Okay," Reuben said.

That proved to me how badly he wanted to play for the Oil Kings: more than he feared flying.

"But that's the not the biggest problem," he continued. "The big problem is why I need to go to Aklavik in the first place."

"Which is?"

"I'm not eighteen," he said. "I need a letter of permission for me to play for the Oil Kings."

My eyes opened wide.

"Oy," I said. I felt like rubbing my own neck.

"*Oy*? Is that like *hence*?"

"Nope," I answered. "It's a short way to say we're in trouble."

25

There was only one person who could sign that letter for him. His legal guardian, Grandma Nellie, who lived in Aklavik.

"You're right," Reuben said. He blew air from his mouth. "Oy, oy, oy."

chapter five

Headsets in place, Buddy George and I were harnessed in our seats at the front of the Beechcraft. Reuben was behind me in one of the passenger seats.

Buddy and I had done all the preflight checks of the aircraft. We made sure that all the flaps were working and that the engine was fine. We'd gone through a takeoff checklist of all our gauges, especially fuel and oil. We'd filed a flight plan. We'd confirmed the weather at Aklavik.

You see, the biggest part of flying safely is to avoid putting yourself in a dangerous flying situation. Good pilots can fly out of bad situations. Great pilots don't allow those situations to happen.

Which is why we still had not begun to taxi into position for takeoff.

A large cargo plane had just taken off. The air currents behind it would be very bumpy. We wanted to make sure we'd take off into smooth air.

Buddy spoke to the tower operator to confirm our position. We were next for takeoff.

Buddy was a big man with a broad face, a white mustache and white hair. He was in his mid-fifties and had been flying since he was my age. He was a great teacher too.

A few minutes later, we were good to go.

We taxied downwind until we reached the end of the runway. We turned into the wind. There were two good reasons for taking off into the wind. It added airspeed.

If the wind was twenty miles an hour into us, we would need that much less speed to take off. The second reason was that we would need less runway to get to lift speed.

Here at the airport in Inuvik, that wasn't a big issue. The runway, at an elevation of 224 feet above sea level, was 6,000 feet long. Well over a mile. The Beechcraft only needed 2,500 feet of runway to get airborne.

"This one's yours," Buddy said into the headset.

I gave him a thumbs-up.

I made sure the nose of the plane was positioned straight down the center of the runway. I released the brakes and gradually pulled the throttle back to give power. Too fast and the plane could swing off center. I made sure the toes and balls of my feet were on the rudder pedals as I started the takeoff roll.

As our speed increased, I felt more pressure on the elevators, which were the flaps at the rear that caused a plane to go up or down. This was good. The plane was getting closer to being controlled by its wings instead of its wheels.

I gradually added pressure to the elevators, which raised the nose slightly. I didn't want to raise it too high. This would spoil the airflow over the wings and put us in danger of a stall.

As we began to leave the ground, I concentrated on keeping the best angle of upward attack. Again, the danger was in rising so quickly that the air would hit the bottom of the wings instead of flowing over them. I also made sure I kept the wings horizontally level.

Our wheels were off the ground. Our speed picked up quickly.

So did my heart rate. To me, this sense of freedom was one of the best feelings in the world.

I maintained takeoff power on the initial climb until we were 500 feet above the ground, not climbing too quickly, but keeping the same upward angle as takeoff.

As we approached our cruising altitude of 2,000 feet, I relaxed.

We intended to fly low enough to enjoy our flight over the Mackenzie River delta.

Inuvik was sixty-two miles upstream from where the Mackenzie flowed into the Arctic Ocean. Far to the south, the Mackenzie was a huge wide river in a single channel of deep dark power. Here in the delta, the Mackenzie was broken up into dozens of shallow channels as it spread through a marshy area about sixty miles wide. For the water to get here, it began 2,600 miles away, where the head rivers of the Peace and Athabasca Rivers flowed into Great Slave Lake. From there, Great Slave fed the Mackenzie, where the main river flowed over 1,000 miles to get to Inuvik. We were flying over water that emptied most of northwestern Canada.

It was an incredible sight from the air. Small lakes and snake-like channels. In the winter, it was a mosaic of white and the dull green of small spruce. Now, it was emerald green and sparkling blue, dotted with the occasional black of a grizzly or moose.

I loved the view.

I looked back to see if Reuben was enjoying it too.

He wasn't. His eyes were scrunched shut. He was sitting like he'd been frozen into position. I couldn't understand why anybody would be afraid of something as cool as flying, but I did feel sorry for him.

Trouble was, it would only get worse in Aklavik.

He still had to face Grandma Nellie.

Oy, oy, oy.

chapter six

The Aklavik runway was 3,000 feet long and twenty-three feet above sea level.

Buddy had taken over the controls, and he landed the Beechcraft without a bump.

From the airport building, we called for the town's taxi, and it was there in minutes. Buddy stayed at the airport, waving for me and Reuben to go ahead. We didn't have to give the taxi driver an address. Just two words: Nellie Reuben.

He took us through the community of about six hundred people.

Aklavik is the Inuvialuit's word for the barren-ground grizzly. The community began when the Hudson's Bay Company opened a trading post in 1912. Because it was on the Peel Channel of the Mackenzie delta, it became a hub for travel. But the Peel Channel flooded too often, so the government decided to move the entire town across the delta and start a new town. It half worked.

The new town was Inuvik, which grew and grew. But some people refused to leave Aklavik, and it didn't become a ghost town. Aklavik was famous for being the place where, in the 1930s, the RCMP tried to catch Albert Johnson, the Mad Trapper of Rat River.

And then—

"We're here," Reuben said, cutting into my thoughts. "Grandma Nellie's."

She lived in a small square house at the edge of the community. It overlooked the river and was surrounded by spruce trees.

Reuben and I took our time getting out of the cab. It might have been easier to face the Mad Trapper.

Grandma Nellie was the same age Reuben's grandfather would have been if he was still alive. They were both born in 1933. Mike Reuben, his grandfather, had died in a snowmobile accident in the seventies. Nellie had never remarried. She was short, her aged skin darkened by years of exposure to sun and cold. She wore traditional Inuvialuit clothing that she made herself from skins. She smelled faintly of animal grease.

Grandma Nellie wanted Reuben to remember the traditional ways. She didn't like him spending time watching television or listening to an iPod. Because Reuben wasn't yet eighteen and because she was his and Lizzie's legal guardian, she could make life difficult for him.

"Hello, Grandma Nellie," Reuben said.

"I see you've brought your friend," Grandma Nellie said. "The one who is not Inuit or Inuvialuit."

"Please," Reuben said, "he is our guest."

All of us sat on wooden cane chairs. There wasn't a television in the cabin. Just a radio.

"So we must keep secrets in front of guests?" Grandma Nellie snapped. "That is far ruder than honest discussion."

It was good, in a way, that Grandma Nellie didn't hide the fact that she wished Reuben had different friends—Inuit friends. It meant I didn't need to take it personally. Grandma Nellie simply saw me as a person who would take Reuben further away from traditional ways than he already was.

"I'm fine with that," I said. "So how's this for honesty: Reuben needs more than just traditional skills. The North is changing, and he has to be ready for it."

"Gear boy, I don't need to listen to you." Grandma Nellie scowled at me. "You have no sense of heritage. Reuben needs to understand where he came from before he can learn where to go."

I should have been more scared of her, but I liked her for her honesty and spunk. Grandma Nellie had the energy of someone half her age. She still trapped. There were animal skins drying on the inside wall of her house. Other people had paintings or photos. Grandma Nellie had splayed-out martins and muskrat. To dry a pelt, you stretched it over a long board the size of the pelt. There was a large beaver pelt on the wall that had been there for years.

I pointed at the old beaver pelt. "How come you haven't sold that one yet?"

"None of your business," Grandma Nellie said to me. "You always did ask too many questions."

"What are you afraid to ask me today?" Grandma Nellie said to Reuben.

"Afraid?" he echoed.

"That's why you always bring this Gear boy. Someone to hide behind?"

Grandma Nellie didn't wait for an answer. She turned away and walked across the small cabin to a stove. She poured water into a kettle and put it on the stove.

Reuben bowed his head and shook it in defeat. He wasn't afraid of anyone in the world—except her.

Grandma Nellie came back to us and sat on her chair as she waited for the water to boil.

"Ask," she said to Reuben. "You want to play hockey down south. So go ahead and ask permission."

It was as if she'd slapped him across the back of the head. "You know?"

"Of course I know," she said. "News travels fast. And you are a very good athlete. Just like your grandfather."

"Don't forget I'm a great athlete too," I said. "Reuben and I scored six goals against the Oil Kings."

No need to point out he'd scored five of them.

Grandma Nellie glared at me. I smiled back. Sweetly.

Secretly, I thought she might actually like me too. Because I was stubborn like her and didn't let her scare me too much.

"Reuben," Grandma Nellie said, "you need me to sign a letter to allow you to play for the Oil Kings. I think that's the real reason you are here."

He knew better than to lie to her. "Yes."

"Then let me surprise you," she said. "I will sign it."

"Huh?" Reuben said. "Without lecturing me about traditional ways and how a person can lose his soul in the south?"

"No," she said, "the letter doesn't come free. You will have to do something."

"I knew it," he said. "What do you want me to do? Build an igloo? Skin a caribou?"

"Nothing like that. You make me a promise. And you keep it."

"What's the promise?" Reuben asked.

The water came to a boil. Grandma Nellie went back to the stove to pour it in a teapot. She came back with three mugs of tea.

I looked at the mug of tea she gave me. "Did you poison this?"

She glared at me again. "I don't think there's enough poison to shut up someone like you." Then she actually did smile. "You are a good friend for Reuben. I want you to help him keep his promise."

"What's the promise?" I was just as suspicious as Reuben.

"When he turns eighteen," Grandma Nellie said, "in the eyes of the law he will be free to make his own decisions. I won't be able to stop him from going south. So no sense trying now. Someday, sooner or later, I won't be here to remind him again and again and again to respect the past."

Respect the past. She wasn't saying anything that Reuben and I hadn't heard before.

"You can go south now," Grandma Nellie said to Reuben. "But you must promise that on your return you will seek the truth about how your grandfather died."

"But you always told me he died in a snowmobile accident," Reuben said, puzzled.

"There is more to it than that," she said. "Much more."

"Like what?"

Grandma Nellie shook her head. "Only when you are ready for the journey. Not while your heart is divided between north and south."

"At least tell me how I'll get started on the journey," Reuben said. "I mean, what if it's not for a few years and by then you are—"

"I'm dead?" Grandma Nellie smiled. That was twice. I'd never seen her smile before this morning. It was a beautiful smile. "That's a sensible question. I'm not young. Don't worry. This is an important journey. It will wait until you are ready."

"I can make that promise," Reuben said firmly. "And I can keep it."

She patted his arm. "You have no idea what it will be worth to you."

chapter seven

"Sorry, dude," Reuben said. "Can't do it again. Can't get on a plane."

Only a couple of hours had passed since getting back from Aklavik. We were sitting in the restaurant at the front of the airport in Inuvik, waiting for the commercial flight to Edmonton. Outside the window, a marten darted in circles, looking for sandwich crusts. Martens were a little bigger than squirrels. But a lot tougher.

Not much else to see. Not a whole lot of traffic outside. All the people for the commercial flight had arrived long before. And since the Canadian North flight was still a few minutes from landing, there were no passengers heading into town. In Inuvik, it's not like commercial flights came and left all the time.

I gave Reuben a sympathetic smile. This was the tenth time he'd mentioned he was afraid.

"I was barely able to get on the charter to Aklavik," he said. "But I wanted hockey more than I was afraid. As we flew back to Inuvik, with each minute sitting there, I got more and more afraid. My brain tells me that it's all right, but everything else screams that I'm going to die. I'm telling you, I could hardly breathe. Flying back nearly killed me."

He clutched my arm. "And it's like my body is still having aftershocks. You know? Like it got hit by an earthquake. But then the little quakes keep hitting."

"Tremors," I said.

"Yeah, tremors. Remember a half hour ago when you left me here to go to the bathroom? I started getting afraid all over again. I don't know if I'll ever be able to sleep again. I can barely walk. I'm glad you're all right with sitting here with me until I feel better."

Out the window, I saw someone I'd been looking for. And my own heart went into tremors. The girl's long dark hair framed a face that was sweet and beautiful and mysterious all at the same time.

Reuben's sister, Lizzie, was walking toward the airport building from the cab that had just dropped her off. It was a beautiful late-summer day, and she had just made it more beautiful.

"About that," I said to Reuben. "I didn't exactly just use the bathroom."

"Huh?"

"I made a couple of phone calls," I said.

I pointed at Lizzie.

"My sister?" Reuben groaned. "You didn't tell her I freaked out, did you?"

"Not yet," I said.

"Not yet?" Reuben began to scowl at me.

"Hear me out," I told him. "I made two calls. The first was to MacDelta Air. Asking my boss for a favor."

"What kind of favor? A baseball bat so you could knock me out and put me out of my misery for a while?"

"He called a friend here at Canadian North to see if they had any extra seats open on the flight south today." If it had been a Friday, there'd have been no chance. On Friday afternoons the planes south were as crowded as they were on Mondays on the planes north. But Saturdays...

"Doesn't matter how many seats are open," Reuben said. He hugged himself as he shivered. "Told you. I'm never flying again."

Lizzie still had about thirty seconds to get inside the airport. I had to talk fast.

"We found two extra seats," I said. "A favor to my boss for favors he's done for his friend. The seats are like sponsor seats. People at Canadian North heard about you getting a shot with the Oil Kings. They want to help."

"One seat or three seats doesn't matter to me. I am not flying. Ever."

"One seat is for me," I said. "I'm going to sit beside you and answer each and every question you have about flying. Once you understand how safe it is, you can relax."

"I told you, no matter what my brain thinks, my body—"

"I understand," I said. "I want to help you make it to Edmonton. But I'd rather ram my face into a porcupine's butt than hold your hand for the entire trip south. That's why there's another seat. I'll be on one side. You'll sit in the middle. And your sister will sit on the other side. She can hold your hand when you need it."

That gave me an idea. Maybe someday I could pretend to be scared enough to want her help. But not today. Reuben needed her.

"My sister," he said. "That's low. You told her how much of a coward I am?"

I smiled. "Really low. But I haven't told her. Yet."

Then I pointed over Reuben's shoulder at Lizzie, who was just stepping into the restaurant, pulling her suitcase.

"It's even worse," I said to Reuben. "When I called her, I told her that you wanted her to come to Edmonton too. So if you cancel, you'll be canceling her trip too. And you know how badly she wants to see the city."

I stood.

Reuben stood. He stomped my toes.

I tried not to hop in pain as Lizzie left her suitcase at the door and ran forward and threw her arms around Reuben. It would have been great for her to hug me but only if I wasn't her brother. Which I wasn't. Which, of course, was why she didn't hug me. So I figured I liked not being her brother and not being hugged more than I would like getting a hug if I were Reuben.

Those thoughts made me want to pound my forehead with the heel of my hand. Why did my brain always have to work in such complicated circles?

She pushed herself away.

"Reuben! Reuben! Reuben!" She was so excited that she couldn't help jumping up and down. "It was so cool of you to get me a ticket to fly to Edmonton with you. You're the best brother ever! This is going to be the best weekend of my life."

Reuben coughed. "Well," he said, "I'm not sure if—"

She jumped and hugged him again. "Thank you! Thank you! Thank you!"

She pushed away and smiled at him. What a beautiful smile.

Reuben glared at me. Didn't matter. Her smile was like the sun, so bright that his dark glare couldn't compete.

"That's right," I said to Reuben. "You're the best brother ever. I'll bet going to

Edmonton will be like Christmas for Lizzie."

She squeezed Reuben again and planted a kiss on his forehead. Which led me again to that whole chain of thought about not being her brother. When she let go again, Reuben took a deep breath.

"Thanks for coming, Lizzie," he said, putting a brave smile on his face. "It's gonna be awesome."

chapter eight

The view from our seats in Edmonton's Rexall Place was fantastic. Below us, the Oil Kings were just getting ready for the opening face-off against the Red Deer Rebels. Reuben Reuben was at right wing. There'd already been articles in the *Edmonton Journal* and *Edmonton Sun* about him.

Here he was, an unknown, brought down from the high Arctic, given a one-game shot to make the Oil Kings. A lot of people would be watching him closely.

Lizzie sat beside me. We were armed with unbuttered popcorn and bottles of water. I would have liked a nice big cup of Coke to wash down the popcorn, plus a chocolate bar for dessert. Okay, two chocolate bars. And it would have been nice to have popcorn on the butter. I mean, butter on the popcorn.

But Lizzie thought it was stupid to eat all those empty calories. I had quickly agreed with her. If Lizzie had said it was stupid to think the sun rose in the east, I would also have agreed with her.

Now, with the game about to start, my heart felt like it was soaring. My best friend was about to prove what a great hockey player he was. And Lizzie was beside me.

I wondered if I should try to impress her with a joke. I knew a really good one about a truck driver and a chimpanzee in diapers...

But before I could start telling it, Lizzie took my hand for a second.

"I want to thank you," she said. "You went to a lot of trouble to help Reuben get this chance."

She didn't let go of my hand.

Maybe I could wait with the joke.

Especially because the ref had just dropped the puck.

I'd been hoping that Godzilla would be the center for Reuben, but I hadn't seen him anywhere in warm-ups. Instead, the Oil Kings' center was a smaller guy named Lankin.

Lankin fought hard for the puck and kicked it over to Reuben. Reuben bounced it back to the Oil Kings' right defenseman. Then Reuben broke for an open spot on the ice, looking for a pass.

The right defenseman fed it to Reuben.

I was already wincing in pain.

From our viewpoint in the stands, it was clear that the pass should never have gone to Reuben. A Rebels' defenseman, as big as Godzilla, had anticipated the pass and had moved up to bodycheck him. By making that terrible pass, the Oil Kings' defenseman had set Reuben up for a monstrous hit. Reuben was looking back for the puck and never saw it coming.

Boom. The Rebels' defenseman threw his hip into Reuben.

Reuben flipped end over end, landing on his helmet and tumbling across the blue line.

Lizzie squeezed my hand so hard one of her nails cut through my palm.

The play continued because the puck had slid into the Rebels' zone. Reuben got to his knees as he was sliding, then onto his skates. But he was wobbling.

"Stupid Eskimo!" shouted a guy sitting directly in front of us. "Go back to your igloo, you loser!" The guy wore a black T-shirt. Muscles bulged from his neck. He was probably ten years older than me.

Lizzie squeezed my hand even harder.

I bit my lip in anger.

Reuben had managed to get back into the flow of the play. The Rebels' defenseman who had knocked him down had picked up the puck. Then he got careless and flipped a cross-ice pass through the air toward a Rebels' winger.

Reuben reached out with his stick and tapped the puck down perfectly. That was his first motion, so smooth it hardly seemed to have happened. His next motion was equally smooth. As the puck flattened on the ice, Reuben set his body and hammered a slap shot through the goalie's legs.

It took a second for the players to figure out what happened. Then another second for the crowd to realize it. But as the goal light turned red, Rexall Place erupted in a huge roar.

It took about thirty seconds for things to settle down.

When it did, I tapped the beefy guy in front of me on the shoulder. He half turned. His face was greasy from the hamburger he was stuffing into his mouth.

"Thought I'd let you know," I said, "Reuben Reuben is not an Eskimo. Only an ignorant person would use that term."

Greasy Face became red face.

"Are you calling me ignorant?" Bits of hamburger bun splattered the air.

"Just helping you out," I said. "Reuben is Inuit. The Inuit of the western Arctic are called Inuvialuit. Farther south, you'll find Gwich'in and Sahtu. See. Now that I've explained, you're not ignorant." I paused. "At least when it comes to this. I'm not sure about your nasty habit of talking with your mouth full."

Greasy Face stood and turned to me. I didn't care. I was angry. I didn't even care that his arms were thicker than my legs.

"I'm going to shut your mouth," he said. "And I'm going to shut it good. Let's see how your Eskimo girlfriend likes that."

Something inside me exploded. Without thinking, I drew my arm back to swing as hard as I could.

I never got the chance to swing. Someone from the side rammed a shoulder into me. As I lost my balance, I was lifted off my feet and held in the air.

chapter nine

The new attacker held me by my shoulders, my feet off the ground. He had dark hair and dark eyes. A big nose. A dark mustache. And a big friendly grin.

Godzilla?

He gently set me on my feet. "Reuben told me where you guys were sitting. I'm out of the game to make room for him to play. So I thought I'd visit and say hi. Looks like I got here just in time."

The people in the stands around us were watching very carefully. Nobody complained that we were blocking their view. This looked like it was going to be a huge show-down. A fight in the stands would be great entertainment.

"Back off," Greasy Face snarled at Godzilla.

They looked like they'd be an even match. But I could make a difference.

"Two against one," I said to Greasy Face. "Do I need to explain the math, or can you figure it out yourself?"

Bad move. Two other men stood. They'd been sitting beside Greasy Face. They were just as big.

"Try the math again," Greasy Face said with a satisfied smile. "You and fancy pants are going to regret this."

Godzilla was wearing a suit and tie. He did look like fancy pants. He reached into his suit jacket and pulled out a cell phone. He flipped it open and handed it to Lizzie.

"Make sure you get this on video," he told Lizzie. "Just point and shoot."

Lizzie nodded.

"Hey," one of Greasy Face's friends said, "it's Kyle Elmore. He plays for the Oil Kings."

Godzilla—Kyle Elmore—smiled at them. "Hello, gentleman. Tell you what, I'll hold off my killer friend here if you stay out of this."

I'm not sure that Godzilla really meant that I was a killer, because both of Greasy Face's friends laughed and sat down.

"I don't care who you are," Greasy Face told Godzilla.

"Don't be stupid," Godzilla told Greasy Face. "I'm not going to fight. If you throw a punch, you'll look like a weenie. And the cops will have all they need on video."

"Hiding behind an Eskimo broad?" Greasy Face sneered.

"Like he told you," Godzilla said. "Inuvialuit. Or Gwich'in. Or Sahtu. Great people."

"Bunch of stupid Eskimos."

"Nice," Godzilla said. "That's going to look good on YouTube, isn't it? What's your name?"

Greasy Face frowned. "Huh?"

"Brave man, insulting a teenage girl in the hockey stands. Let's have your name so the world can know it. Speak clearly into the camera."

"Shut up," Greasy Face said, starting to squirm. He put his hand up to block the phone's camera.

It seemed like we were in a private bubble. I'd almost forgotten we were in the stands of Rexall Place, but I was reminded a second later that this was a hockey game. An exciting hockey game.

The crowd erupted with another huge roar.

It distracted all of us.

Godzilla motioned for Lizzie to hand him back the cell phone.

When the crowd settled, Greasy Face was still standing.

"You notice that?" Godzilla said to Greasy Face. "Scored by Reuben Reuben. His second goal of the shift. How about I erase the video on this camera and all of us just enjoy watching him play."

"Sure," Greasy Face said, his face red. "That Eskimo—I mean Inuit—guy is a great player."

chapter ten

After that exhibition game in Edmonton, Reuben stayed in Edmonton to play for the Oil Kings, and Lizzie and I flew back to Inuvik.

We didn't see him until the Christmas break four months later. During those four months, the Oil Kings had managed to dominate the league, and Reuben had done the same to the scoring race.

We were waiting at the airport for him

a couple of days before Christmas. A sideways wind blew snow across the delta.

Lizzie and I stood by a window overlooking the runway. The trees on the other side were barely visible through the blowing snow.

The airport in Inuvik didn't have gates. Just a door where people walked in from the airplane. Reuben was the first off the Canadian North plane, and Lizzie kept waving at him as he walked across the tarmac. I only waved once. It's a guy thing.

Reuben gave us a big grin as he walked inside.

She hugged him.

I didn't. Another guy thing.

"Good to see you both," Reuben said.

"Yup," I said. "Godzilla on the plane too?"

"Yup. At the back."

There was a reason that Godzilla had been invited to come to Inuvik.

He and Reuben were going to become YouTube stars.

From the airport, we took my old Toyota directly down Mackenzie Road to the small downtown area. We had an appointment with a lawyer named Philip Collins. He was a trusted man in this small town. Everybody knew he was honest and that he cared about people more than he did about money. He was also Reuben's hockey agent.

The four of us—Lizzie, Reuben, Godzilla and I—sat down in his office.

Philip Collins was old enough to retire. He looked like the colonel from KFC, and he wore a bow tie too. His shiny old suit had flakes of dandruff on the shoulders.

"Good to see you," Philip said. He was sorting through some mail on his desk. I knew why Reuben and Godzilla had been invited, and I knew Lizzie was here because she was Reuben's sister. It was a mystery why I was here.

Philip didn't waste any time answering my silent question.

"Gear," he said to me, "you're needed because you can play hockey and because you can help fly."

"I hate flying," Reuben said. "Half the reason I play so hard for the Oil Kings is because I know as long as I'm on the team, I don't have to get on a jet to come home again."

"Exactly," Philip said. "This documentary is a big deal. Gear's your best friend. He'll do everything to make the flying part easier on you. Right, Gear?"

I hardly heard the question. What had Philip meant about hockey?

"Gear?"

"I'm playing hockey?" I said.

"You're a decent player," Philip answered. "And you're local."

Reuben gave me a high five. But I still didn't understand.

"I've been over this with Reuben on the phone already," Philip said. "But let me go over it again so everybody is on the same page."

We nodded. Godzilla stretched and smiled.

"Just down the hall," Philip said, "is the office of Matlock Construction." He laughed and pointed at the mail he'd sorted. "We're so close we often get each other's mail."

He didn't have to explain anything about Matlock Construction. Danny Matlock had come to Inuvik a few years earlier and ran one of the biggest construction companies in town.

"Danny came to me with a great idea," Philip said. "A three-on-three pond-hockey tournament. Matlock Construction is putting up the money to tour all the western Arctic communities. And he's donating the prize money too. It's going to cost him a lot, but he wants to put money back into the communities."

I still didn't see how I fit in.

"The Oil Kings have given this their blessing," Philip continued. "Because it's a three-on-three format, they know there's not much chance Reuben's going to get hurt."

True. Three-on-three tournaments were supposed to be high scoring with lots of action. No body checks. No slap shots. No offsides.

"It's the perfect showcase for Reuben's talents," Philip said. "When Matlock first brought the idea to me in late November, we agreed it would be important that someone in each community film each game. By the time the tour is finished, it should make for an amazing highlight reel that will give Reuben great exposure on television, but also on the Internet. Being on YouTube should help him when it comes to negotiating a professional hockey contract."

I was surprised that someone as old as Philip had any idea about YouTube, but it wouldn't be smart to say that.

"It's also great publicity for the western Arctic," Philip said. "People in the south are going to learn about all the communities up here. So you can see there is a lot at stake. But we're going to have to fly from community to community. You, Gear, know that as well as anyone. And Reuben hates flying. He wants you along for that."

Reuben grinned at me.

"Didn't you say something about hockey?" I asked.

"We can use you," Godzilla told me. "You're pretty good at winning a draw. That's important in this format."

"You all know the pond-hockey format," Philip said. "Three against three for four periods of five minutes each. This three-on-three setup is perfect for a lot of reasons. First, it allows Reuben to play during the Christmas break without worrying about injury, and it showcases his talents. Second, the communities are too small to assemble a full team for regular hockey exhibitions. Three-on-three hockey gives each community a chance to put some strong talent on the ice. And lastly, Matlock wants to keep the costs down. You can imagine the difference in expenses between sending out a twenty-player team and a three-player team."

I could. Hotel rooms in the remote communities could be as high as three hundred dollars a night. Sixteen extra players would cost Matlock nearly five thousand dollars extra per night. Restaurant food was expensive in the North. And chartering a big enough airplane for twenty players would cost a fortune.

Obviously, Matlock was a smart man.

"Gear," Philip said, "you can help as copilot and also keep Reuben from going crazy with fear during flights. But we know you're a good enough hockey player to be the third man. And you and Reuben can share a room. That saves Matlock the cost of a hotel room in each community."

"So how much is he paying me for the tour?" I joked.

"I negotiated five thousand toward your pilot training," Philip said. "Double if your team goes undefeated. That enough?"

"Let me think about it," I said. I thought for half a second. "Yup, I'm fine with it."

There was a knock on the door, but before Philip could get up to answer, a man pushed it open.

"Good to see you, Danny," Philip said. "They got our mail mixed up again." He stood and handed the letters he'd set aside to the man who had just walked into the room.

Danny Matlock was about fifty years old. He was big, with graying red hair and a red beard. He wore a flannel shirt, suspenders, jeans and work boots. He had three down-filled coats tucked under his arm. He took the mail from Philip and stuffed it into his back pocket.

"Boys!" he boomed. "Good to see you!"

He held out the coats. One to me. One to Reuben. One to Godzilla.

The Oil Kings logo was on the front of the coats. On the back was a big circle with the name *Matlock* in the middle.

"Philip, you explained everything, right?" Before Philip could answer, Danny boomed, as if he were speaking to a crowd in a gym, "So boys, you wear these at all times, unless you're sleeping. And even then, you better have them nearby. I want my company logo in full view all the time. Understand?"

I understood. For five or ten thousand dollars toward pilot training, I would have been happy to wear a tutu.

chapter eleven

Tuktoyaktuk. North and east of Inuvik.

Simpler to call it Tuk, like everyone else did. We could have taken the ice highway, but that meant hours of slow driving on the Mackenzie River to Kugmallit Bay, where Tuk overlooked the Arctic Ocean. Instead, by air our trip had taken well under an hour. Plus, we needed the Beechcraft to go from Tuk to the next community, because there definitely wasn't any other way to get there.

Flying into Tuk, I always looked for pingos. There were over a thousand in the area. They looked like mini volcanoes. They were mounds of earth-covered ice that existed only where there was permafrost.

The name Tuktoyaktuk was an Inuvialuit name that meant "looks like a caribou." According to legend, a woman saw some caribou wade into the water and turn into stone. In the summer, at low tide, reefs that looked like petrified caribou could be seen in the water. Tuk was a place the Inuvialuit had used for centuries to harvest caribou and beluga whales.

I focused on landing. The runway length was five thousand feet. Gravel surface but hard-packed snow in the winter. Elevation: fifteen feet above sea level.

As we came in on final approach, all of Tuk flashed below us. We were north of the tree line. There was a purity of whiteness that stretched in all directions around the scattering of houses. In the summer, it would have been different.

To the north: the blue of the Arctic Ocean. To the south: the pingos and open rolling green terrain.

I put the Beechcraft down so smoothly, it felt like a marble rolling across a glass tabletop.

"Good job," Buddy said in the headset.

I nodded.

I sure hoped my hockey playing was as smooth.

Outside the rink, the wind had not been blowing, but it was still minus thirty.

Inside, of course, it was a lot warmer. The rink was so packed with fans it probably didn't even need any heaters.

I'm sure they were watching for a couple of reasons. First, Reuben Reuben was on the ice. As soon as he began warm-ups, they all cheered. The noise shook the building like a freight train. Second—or maybe first— the fans made it clear they loved the home team from Tuk. There were four players.

Two were about our age. Two were in their late twenties. The rules were simple: three skaters for each team on the ice at a time. That meant the Tuk team could rotate, leaving one person on the bench to rest while the other three played.

We only had the three of us. With four periods of five minutes each, that meant we were at a disadvantage, offset by the fact that we had Reuben and Godzilla on our team. It was going to be a close game.

And that was probably the third reason that nearly everybody from Tuk was in the stands. Danny Matlock had set up the tour to make it as exciting as possible. If the home team won, Matlock Construction would donate $5,000 to the local hockey program. The money could be used for equipment, tournaments and travel. If our team won, he would donate only $2,000 to the community hockey program, and the other $3,000 would go to Reuben Reuben's favorite charity, a foundation that helped kids with terminal illnesses fulfill their dreams.

Each town would supply two goalies. The goalies would switch after each period, so each team would have each goalie for two periods. To make sure that the goalies wouldn't favor the home team and let in easy goals, Matlock Construction was going to give a large flat-screen television to the goalie that let in the fewest goals.

I soaked up the sights and sounds as I warmed up in our end. Playing WHL hockey wasn't a dream for me; I wanted to be a pilot. Because I'd never play hockey at Reuben or Godzilla's level, this was as close as I'd get.

And I was nervous. Not only was the crowd here to see every mistake I made, but, as Matlock had requested, there were four kids in the stands armed with video cameras. They were here to catch the action. Later, the four videos from each community would be sent to an agency that would use the raw footage to put together some highlight reels.

I must have looked as nervous as I felt. Godzilla whacked my butt with the blade of his stick as he skated past me. "Get rid of the frown, buddy. We're going to make this fun. And remember what I said. You're about as good at taking a draw as anyone I've played against. The rest of your game could use work, but you're magic in the face-off circle."

"Sure." My mouth was dry. I wanted warm-ups to continue for another couple of hours. But thirty seconds later the ref blew the whistle to start the game. I had no choice but to step into the face-off circle at center ice.

We had decided this earlier. We were going to set up like a lopsided triangle. Me at the front. Reuben behind my left side, halfway between the centerline and our blue line. Godzilla took his place behind me on the right but closer to the net than Reuben, almost on our blue line. That meant a lot depended on me to win the draw and get the puck moving back toward our net. If we were able to take immediate control of the puck, we could fire up the offense. But if I lost the draw, we'd have two men caught deep, and Tuk would be able to attack. With only three skaters on the ice, this game was all about offense. Not defense.

The ref's hand flashed downward with the puck. I won the face-off clean, pulling the puck straight back to Reuben. He skated backward with the puck, drawing one of the Tuk players, who looked like he wanted to impress the crowd. Reuben kept pedaling backward, drawing the second Tuk player too.

I saw this clearly, because I was waiting well inside the Tuk blue line. Pond-hockey rules. No slap shots, no body contact.

And no offsides.

Godzilla cut across the ice, wide open. That drew the third Tuk player, who was forced to guard Godzilla. I was as alone as if I had used skunk spray for deodorant.

From beside our net, Reuben fired a knee-high slap shot between the two Tuk players and onto on my stick blade.

Here was my chance to open with a goal!

Except I knew I wasn't a goal scorer.

Godzilla was though.

The Tuk player guarding him peeled away to try to stop me. I stayed wide of the net as I headed down the ice, drawing the Tuk player even farther to the boards. Then I flipped the puck back toward center. A nice soft floating pass that Godzilla scooped up and snapped between the goalie's legs.

He raised his arms as the crowd cheered.

"See?" he said, rubbing my helmet as he skated up to me. "Easy as pie."

Best of all, we'd stuck to our plan, which was to move the puck around by passing instead of carrying it. It made the Tuk players do a lot more skating.

We managed to stick with the game plan. Out of thirty-five draws, I won twenty-nine of them.

We won 15–9.

And I was that much closer to my ten-thousand-dollar scholarship.

chapter twelve

"Good game," Eddie said. His skin was the color of dark walnut. "It was fun to watch."

We didn't know why Eddie had stopped in the dressing room and asked us to meet him at the Tuk school after the game. We just knew it would have been very rude to say no. Eddie was a respected elder in the community. So Reuben, Godzilla and I sat with Eddie in the library of Mangilaluk School in Tuktoyaktuk. The government people who put posters in the tiny airport terminals of the western Arctic sure could have learned from this school. It had wonderful colorful posters that would cheer anyone up.

"Before we talk," Eddie said, "we eat. Follow me."

He took us to the warm staff room. Delicious smells filled the air.

"Traditional foods," Eddie said to Reuben. "The food that I ate when I was a boy. And when your grandmother was young."

Reuben made a face.

Eddie shook his head.

"Too much sugar in what your generation eats," Eddie said. "It destroys our health. When I was young, the food we ate gave us strength."

Eddie pointed outside. "To any other people, that land out there is nothing but wind and snow. And death. We lived through each winter. We had strength. Now eat. Then I'll tell you what you came for."

What we came for? It didn't make sense. He'd asked to meet with us.

Reuben shrugged.

I wasn't looking forward to it, but the tastes surprised me in a pleasant way. *Muktuk*—seal blubber. Smoked caribou. Char.

I was hungrier than I'd expected. I looked up and noticed that Reuben had finished at the same time. Godzilla had gone back for third and fourth helpings. That left me and Reuben alone with Eddie.

Eddie smiled. It lit up his ancient face.

"Now your body is prepared to go outside and walk for miles in a blizzard," Eddie said. "I only wish your grandfather had been prepared with food like this to help him make it through a blizzard."

Reuben frowned too. "Blizzard?"

"It's how he died," Eddie said.

"But I was told it was a snowmobile accident on one of the delta channels outside of Aklavik."

"Were you told the RCMP were chasing him?" Eddie asked.

Reuben looked shocked. "What?"

"Someone from the south called the RCMP and told them to arrest your grandfather. He heard about it. Jumped on his snowmobile. But he didn't have the right clothing or the right food. A blizzard swept through the delta. People are amazed he made it as far as he did. But still, he finally lost his fight against the weather."

"RCMP?" Reuben said. "My grandfather? Why did they want to arrest him?"

Eddie shook his head. "You won't get the answer from me." He reached into his back pocket. "Here is what you were sent to get from me."

"Sent?" Reuben said.

It didn't make sense to me either. Why did Eddie think we had been sent to meet him?

Eddie didn't explain. He handed Reuben a blank envelope.

Reuben opened it and showed me the letter inside. "It's Grandma Nellie's handwriting."

Go to Sachs Harbour. There is A guide. Named JimMy. Meet him at the school.

chapter thirteen

Sachs Harbour is on the coast of Banks Island, overlooking the Amundsen Gulf of the Beaufort Sea. It's the most northern community in the Northwest Territories. Population: 130. Runway: 4,000 feet. Elevation: 282 feet above sea level. I knew Sachs Harbour was named after one of the ships in the Canadian Artic Expedition of 1913. But I liked its traditional name, Ikaahuk, better. It means "where you go across to."

Remote? Food and supplies reached Sachs Harbour by barge in the few short summer months. It was a tough place to spend the winter if you didn't see beauty in ice and snow.

It was a great place for hunting. Banks Island has the largest goose colony in the world and three-quarters of the world's population of musk ox. A few years earlier, a hunter here shot a grolar bear.

Yeah, you think I got that wrong. But I didn't.

The bear had the long claws and thick creamy white fur you'd expect of a polar bear, but it had the humped back and shallow face of a grizzly, along with brown patches around its eyes, nose and back.

So scientists did DNA tests.

It was a grolar bear—the father was a grizzly bear and the mother, a polar bear.

With my weird brain, I couldn't help but wonder if it would have been better to name it a pizzly bear instead.

We landed at Sachs Harbour well after the end of the short twilight. This far north, the sun never makes it to the horizon. People in the south think that means it's dark twenty-four hours a day, but that's not true. The sun gets close enough to the horizon to give some light, not much stronger than dusk.

The wind had picked up, and I was grateful for the warmth inside the truck that brought us into the community from the airport.

The hockey game seemed to go past very quickly. We won 14-7, even on tired legs after playing earlier in Tuk. Godzilla and Reuben did their usual magic on the ice, and I won most of the draws and tried to stay out of the way. Winning didn't seem nearly as important as the fact that everyone had fun. It was obvious that it was a highlight for the community.

After the game, Buddy and Godzilla went to the hostel, and Reuben and I went by truck to Inualthuyak School. Reuben had asked me to stay with him because he wanted help figuring out what was going on. Why were we supposed to meet a guide named Jimmy?

The wind hurled ice crystals into our faces during the short walk from the truck into the school, and my face burned for a few minutes after we stepped into the warmth. I was surprised when we found a much younger man than Eddie waiting for us inside. And I was even more surprised when he handed us snowsuits and goggles.

"Bundle up," he said. He grinned, showing strong white teeth. There were traces of black skin on his cheeks. Frostbite.

"Wait a minute," Reuben said. "We've got questions about my grandfather. We're supposed to ask for a guide named Jimmy."

"That's me," Jimmy said. "Got a letter for you in my back pocket. But not before we get on a snowmobile."

"Who gave you the letter? Why? What's going on?"

Jimmy ignored the questions. "Only one way to find out. Get on the snowmobile. Want to be stupid about it and not wear this stuff?"

I thought of the hostel where we'd booked a room. I'd been there before. It had satellite television with all the shows from the south. I thought about how warm it would be, how good to get some food, maybe even a steak.

"If this is what it takes," Reuben said.

As we put on the gear, Jimmy checked his rifle to make sure it was oiled. All I could think about was a huge grolar bear somewhere out there. Hungry and waiting. If it ate you, it wouldn't matter whether it was a grolar or a pizzly.

Five minutes later, we went back into the dark and cold, where three snow-mobiles were waiting for us.

Jimmy jumped on his, rifle close by. He started it, and the headlights went on, light bouncing off the ice crystals.

"Stay close!" he shouted above the engine noise. "You don't want to get lost out here!"

I was grateful that we spent only twenty minutes or so following him in a single line. Inside my snowsuit, I was still shivering. Partly because of the cold. And partly because of how alone we seemed out here. It was hundreds of miles to another community. We were on the vastness of an island on the Arctic Ocean, so frozen with ice and packed snow that it was impossible to tell where the land stopped and the ocean began. The wind was blowing so hard that it was destroying our snowmobile tracks. Without Jimmy, Reuben and I would have had no chance of finding our way back.

I was really grateful when Jimmy stopped—and astounded at what we saw in his snowmobile headlights.

Musk ox.

Jimmy's headlights snapped off. In our own headlights, we saw him walk toward us. He reached down and shut off Reuben's snowmobile, then mine.

Silence.

Except for the wind.

Then I heard something else.

The breathing of animals. We were close enough that I could see steam coming from their nostrils. The animals were facing us in a solid wall. Heads lowered. Horns in protective position.

Musk ox are smaller than you might imagine. The biggest males would only reach chest-high on me.

It was eerie that they didn't move. They just formed a wall.

"What don't you see?" Jimmy asked, raising his voice to be heard above the wind.

Reuben didn't answer. I didn't answer. I knew this was a serious question, so I didn't yell that I was glad I didn't see a grolar bear.

I expected Jimmy to answer his own question.

He surprised me yet again. He jumped on his snowmobile and started the engine. He swung the machine around. "Come on," he said. "Start 'em up. I want supper!"

We followed him back to Sachs Harbour. We had spent all this time risking our lives on the wide-open snow for a question with no answer?

I was glad when the lights of the town appeared, small diamonds glittering in a vast, dark and cold landscape.

At the hostel, Jimmy ate without saying a word. Reuben and I did the same. Godzilla was in his room. When Jimmy finished his last bite of steak, he pulled a letter out of his back pocket.

"Your grandfather was a great guide and hunter," Jimmy said. "Your grandmother Nellie is well respected among the elders. I was happy to help her."

"When did you get the letter?" I asked.

"In November," Jimmy said. "She mailed it to me from Aklavik." He handed Reuben the letter.

Reuben opened the envelope and took out a folded piece of paper. It was a newspaper article from the *Vancouver Sun*, dated January 4, 1978. It reported that a man named Mike Reuben was wanted by RCMP in connection with an assault in Vancouver. A complaint had been filed by a man named Reginald Willowby.

Reuben read it. I read it. Reuben read it again.

"That's it?" Reuben asked.

"Almost," Jimmy said.

There was one more piece of paper inside the envelope. Another note from Grandma Nellie. *In Holman, look for an elder nAmed Sarah. She has Good stories.*

"I don't get it," Reuben told Jimmy. "What's all this about?"

"Don't know," Jimmy said pleasantly. "I'm just doing what I was asked."

"Even the trip out to the musk ox?" I asked.

He nodded his head. "You two belong to a different generation. I think there's danger when you forget what your parents and grandparents and the generations before you faced. They lived because they could endure this land. They didn't have parkas and snowmobiles. A hundred years ago, they didn't have rifles. Reuben, you have a great heritage. You need to know about it. And once you know about it, you'll understand that you can take pride in it."

Jimmy pushed away from the table.

What was going on here? Holman was our next stop for the three-on-three pond-hockey tour. The first mystery was what Grandma Nellie was trying to get us to learn. The bigger mystery was how she'd known how the tour would be planned. She'd mailed the letter to Jimmy in November. But the tour had not been finalized until early December. Weird. Very weird.

Reuben asked one last question. "When you brought us to the herd of musk ox, what didn't we see?"

"The young ones behind the adults," Jimmy said. "Wolves and bears can't reach the young ones as long as the adults gather around to protect them. Our elders do that for our young ones. And when it's your turn, you need to do the same."

chapter fourteen

"I'm tired of seeing you shiver like a dog back there," Buddy George told Reuben. "I want you in the copilot seat for the flight."

When we heard that, Godzilla and I screamed like little girls on a roller coaster.

Godzilla might really have been afraid.

But I was fine with it. Some companies that book charters have strict regulations that require two pilots, even though it increases the cost. Other charter flights, however, are booked with only one pilot.

Buddy would be in complete control of the plane, and he'd coach Reuben through every step of the process.

"Me?" Reuben suddenly went rigid. And it wasn't just the cold inside the airplane. Buddy had just started the engines, and it would take a few minutes to warm up.

"You," Buddy said. He pointed at the copilot seat and held out the headphones for Reuben. "You're even going to spend some time flying this."

A snail could have beaten Reuben on his way to the copilot seat. But he finally made it.

I knew what he'd see. The row of lights leading down the runway. The front of the plane lifting.

I only hoped he'd also feel what I felt when the plane rushed forward, gathering speed until the wheels broke free of the ground.

Freedom.

We reached Holman as the first dull light of the day hit the snow and ice. We'd seen a pack of wolves on the approach, and I couldn't help thinking about the musk ox and the quiet solid wall of protection. It took patience and strength and willpower to survive up here. But if you had all three, not even the wolves would get you.

I watched Reuben's body language on the final approach to the airport. He was leaning forward, as if he was interested, not terrified. I could see his mouth moving, but above the noise of the engines I couldn't hear what he was saying. At least he wasn't curled up in terror anymore.

There had been a hard crosswind on the approach, but the aircraft stopped shaking as we dropped in elevation. The nearby hills nearly always funneled the winds directly down the runway. In fact, some days, with snow in the air, you could see a wind line halfway between the airport and town, because the funneling effect of the winds caused the airport to be in a blizzard while the town was clear. And sometimes the opposite happened. You'd land in clear air when the town was hidden in a blizzard.

The wheels touched down with hardly a bump. Runway: 4,300 feet. Elevation: 117 feet above sea level.

We were officially in Holman, on Victoria Island.

But it wasn't called Holman anymore. A couple of years earlier, it had reclaimed the traditional name of Ulukhaktok.

The world's most northern golf course was here, and it had a famous tournament called the Billy Joss Open. The Holman Co-op was a place where people of the community, especially printmakers like Mary Okheena, marketed their arts and crafts to the world. Buddy and Godzilla went to the rink. We had about an hour before the game. It wasn't difficult to find Sarah. The manager at the hotel told Reuben and me that we could find her at Helen Kalvak School.

She was waiting for us with a knife.

"What did you see parked outside the school?" she asked us. She was probably in her sixties. She had a great smile. It bunched her cheeks into wrinkled apples.

"Snowmobiles," Reuben said. Up here, it was no big deal that kids drove their snowmobiles to school. Just like how kids in the south drove cars to school.

"On the way here from the airport, did you see the dog teams too?" she asked.

Reuben nodded.

Ulukhaktok's population was just under four hundred. Many families kept traditional dog teams of huskies. Each dog was on a leash that kept it away from other dogs. In the winter, you could see the bodies of dead caribou just out of reach of the dogs. Every day, the owner would go out with a hacksaw and cut meat off the caribou to feed the dogs.

"The new ways with the traditional ways," Sarah said. "We can hold onto our past without becoming prisoners of it."

She held up the knife. Actually, it was an *ulu*. The bottom was a semicircle. The handle was made of caribou antler. The name Ulukhaktok meant "the place where ulu parts are found," because the bluff that overlooked Ulukhaktok provided slate and copper for the ulus.

"I can skin a caribou with this," she said. "And when I am finished, I can go to a computer in this school and e-mail my friends in other communities. Past and future. Together."

"That sounds exactly like something Grandma Nellie would want me to hear," Reuben said. "Except she's not so excited about the Internet and stuff like that."

"She's a remarkable woman," Sarah said.

"She sent you a letter?" I asked. "In November?"

Sarah nodded. Again, I had to ask myself: How did Grandma Nellie know we would be coming here before the tour had even been planned? And what was it she wanted us to learn? Why string it out like this?

"Nellie wanted me to tell you about Mike Reuben," Sarah said. "I knew him. Many of us in Ulukhaktok have extended family that runs down the Mackenzie delta. Mike Reuben was a great athlete and a skilled hunter. More importantly, he was a man of his word."

"He doesn't sound honest to me. He was running from the RCMP when he died in a blizzard," Reuben said. He quickly added, "I don't mean disrespect to you."

"What else do you know?"

"He fought with a man named Reginald Willowby." Reuben pulled out the newspaper clipping and gave it to her. "That's why the RCMP wanted to arrest him."

"Hmmm." She got up and moved gracefully from the couch in the staff room where we'd been talking. She motioned for us to follow.

We did.

She stopped at a computer in the library. It was quiet. Most kids were in class.

Her fingers flashed as she worked the keyboard. The same fingers that used an ulu to skin caribou.

"Google Maps," she said. "One of my favorite things on the Internet. What was the address in that article?"

Reuben told her.

Seconds later, there it was on a map on the computer screen. She zoomed in, then switched the view from Map to Satellite.

She zoomed in further.

"Look at this. See how the houses are far apart? See how big the roofs are?"

"Sure," Reuben said.

"This is a neighborhood full of rich people. People who can afford to come up to the North and hunt."

That made sense. The guy who had shot the grolar bear near Sachs Harbour had paid fifty thousand dollars for the hunt.

She pointed at the computer screen. "So maybe you find it interesting that this was the house that Mike Reuben visited. Imagine someone like your grandfather as a young man. He can track animals and survive the winters of the North with just a rifle, an ax and matches. But the rich-man's world in Vancouver would be terrifying to him. Yet that's where Mike Reuben went."

"It doesn't make sense," Reuben said.

"Reginald Willowby had been north many times," Sarah told us. "He had a reputation for treating guides bad. For trying to cheat them. One trip in November of 1977, he came north and hired Mike Reuben as a guide. He stayed at Mike Reuben's cabin."

The date of the newspaper article was January 4, 1978.

"Less than two months later," I said, "Mike Reuben went to Vancouver and got into a fight with him."

Sarah nodded. "I heard Willowby had stolen something from him. But nobody knew what."

"My grandfather should have called the police if Willowby stole something from him," Reuben said.

"Unless there was a good reason not to call the police," I said. "The article doesn't mention that anything was stolen. And you would think your grandfather would have told the police. Either in Vancouver or when he was back up north."

We sat in silence for a few moments.

I thought of something else. I looked at Sarah. "You had already planned to show us the house on Google Maps," I said. "Right?"

She just smiled and handed Reuben another note from Grandma Nellie. *In PaUlatuuQ, an elder named Elizabeth will tell you more.*

He put it in his pocket.

"That's all you've got, isn't it?" Reuben said.

"It is," she answered. "Maybe you'll find the rest of it in Paulatuuq."

Paulatuuq was our next stop on the tour.

It couldn't be coincidence. How had Grandma Nellie managed to plan this?

chapter fifteen

Our wheels were up and we were in the air two hours later. In Ulukhaktok, we'd won our third game in a row. I'd scored a couple of goals, and it felt like the three of us were meshing well. On the other hand, a blindfolded seal would have looked good with Reuben and Godzilla as teammates, so I wasn't going to get conceited about my hockey.

In the air, we headed south and west into the wind toward Paulatuuq. In my mind, we were tracing the route of a flat-tened diamond. Look at a map of Canada. Look way north. The western point of the diamond is Tuk. From there, draw a straight line northeast to Sachs Harbour. From there, draw another line south and east to Ulukhaktok, or as it might be on older maps, Holman. Then go south and west to Paulatuuq. The last part of the diamond goes back to Tuk, crossing over the Smoking Hills just west of Paulatuuq. These were cliffs overlooking the Arctic Ocean, made of oil shales. Struck by lightning centuries ago, the hills have been burning slowly ever since, giving off the clouds of smoke that gave the hills and the town their names. The name meant "place of coal."

It was hard to imagine that we'd only left Inuvik the morning of the day before and had played three games in three different communities already. Flying made it all possible. And the weather was holding for us. Sometimes, if a fog settled or the wind blew too hard, these northern airports could be closed for days.

Win or lose, I was looking forward to a good night's sleep.

Just like at the other games, the rink was standing room only, which makes it sound like there were more people than there really were. In the south, there were usually stands on both sides of the ice, and maybe behind both nets too. Not in the North. The arenas were built smaller, and the only stands were opposite the players' benches.

But the fans' side of the ice *was* packed. They loved Reuben. They loved Godzilla. And they loved the home team. Plus, everyone knew that we'd won three in a row. Here in Paulatuuq, it was obvious by the screaming and yelling that they were hoping to be the ones to finally beat us.

The Paulatuuq players took a different approach to the game.

In Tuk, Sachs Harbour and Ulukhaktok, the opposing players had charged around the ice, handling the puck more than passing it. It had proven two things. The players in each community were highly skilled, and their fans loved watching them make great moves with the puck. But it had also proven that passing the puck was easier than carrying it, and Reuben, Godzilla and I had not worn ourselves out. Here, however, it became immediately clear that the Paulatuuq players were going to play as a team instead of as individuals.

They passed just as much as we did. I was still winning more than three-quarters of the draws, which was very helpful. But we were getting tired. They weren't. We went into the fourth five-minute period tied at 10–10. The wide-open offensive game had the fans screaming.

Just before we began the final period, I could see that Reuben and Godzilla were on their last legs.

I called them over to the boards.

"I have an idea," I said. "Right now, you guys are the best players in the entire Arctic. So let's make this a two-on-two game."

"Great idea, Gear," Godzilla said. He was leaning on his knees. Sweat dripped onto the ice. "Go over to the ref and tell him we want the rules changed. While you're at it, let the fans know too. I'm sure everyone will be happy."

"Not like that. We know already who the best goal scorer is on their team." It was number 19, a guy a little bigger than me but not quite as fast. He had great stick-handling skills and a fast wrist shot. Nearly every time I lost the draw, the other two found a way to get him the puck, and he'd either score or set up a pass for a goal. "When he's on the ice, I'll stick closer to him than his own shadow. I won't let him get a sniff at the puck. When I shout for a pass, fake it to me but hold on to it. I need to save my energy when we've got the puck. What do you think about it?"

Reuben grinned. "Love it. Let's go!"

I lost the draw. Instead of following the puck, I went straight to number 19. I didn't even look for the puck. I watched his eyes as he skated. Within seconds, he dropped his head. Again, I didn't look for the puck. I reached down with my stick and trapped his stick beneath the shaft of mine. The puck slid past him. Off the boards. And back to Godzilla.

Reuben was directly across the ice. Godzilla feathered it across to him.

Instead of breaking for open ice like I'd done the previous three periods, I stayed with number 19. I was so close to him I could hear his breathing.

He wheeled to a spot in the neutral zone. I did the same.

Behind our blue line, Reuben passed it back to Godzilla. That brought one of the Paulatuuq players into our zone. He stayed in the middle, so Godzilla couldn't pass it back to Reuben again. But Godzilla moved slowly up the ice. Very slowly. With no one pressuring him, he didn't have to waste energy.

Now it became cat and mouse.

Number 19 made a move to Godzilla.

"Wide open!" I shouted. Godzilla set his body into position to pass it to me. So number 19 drifted back to me to make sure I didn't get the pass.

Which was great for Godzilla. No pressure on him.

Since I was covered, he held on to the puck and drifted a bit closer to their blue line.

Now the pace of the game had slowed completely. The Paulatuuq fans were screaming for something to happen.

The player in the middle broke toward Godzilla, who flipped the puck back to Reuben. Reuben was able to buy another thirty seconds of rest time, slowly moving with the puck.

Number 19 couldn't take it any longer. He dashed toward Reuben.

I slid over to one side. Wide open. Reuben shoveled a pass to me. Number 19 spun to charge me. I banked the puck off the boards back to Reuben. Over a minute had passed, and we hadn't lost control of the puck or moved it across the centerline. But we hadn't done much skating either.

Reuben was rested. He cradled my pass.

Number 19 had spun back toward Reuben, who easily sidestepped him. Then he beat the second Paulatuuq player. Now it was two on one. Reuben and me. Godzilla hadn't moved a step. He was resting.

I cut wide, screaming for the pass.

Reuben grinned. He knew and I knew that there was no way he'd dump the puck off to me.

But it drew the third player.

Reuben waltzed in on the goalie. Faked left. Faked right. Lifted a backhand high into the net.

Goal!

We used the same strategy to score two more goals and kill the last three minutes of the game.

Final score, 13-10 for us.

But it didn't earn me a good night's sleep like I'd hoped. Instead, after winning the fourth out of four games, with Godzilla and Buddy safe and warm in the hotel, Reuben and I spent the night in an igloo. In minus-forty-degree cold.

chapter sixteen

The igloo adventure began just after the game, when an elder named Elizabeth met us at the rink and took us to Angik School. She wasn't the only one waiting for us. When we stepped inside, pulling off our hats and thick coats, Reuben was swarmed by kids.

"Reuben Reuben!" they chanted. "Reuben Reuben! Reuben Reuben!"

It wasn't a total surprise. Angik School was named after a very respected elder. Angik was related to many of Paulatuuq's kids.

And one of them was Reuben Reuben, whose own grandfather was part of this extended family.

"Hey, you rock, man!" one kid said, giving Reuben a high five. "You play for the Oil Kings!"

Reuben gave high fives all around.

Little kids swarmed Godzilla too. He lifted one kid and put him on his shoulders. Another kid jumped on his back. Godzilla pretended the weight made him stagger, and he wobbled in stiff-legged steps that made all the kids laugh.

"Want to see us drum dance?" a girl shyly asked Godzilla.

"Love to," he said.

Reuben nodded too. So did I. The teachers pulled all the kids from class and we assembled in the gym in honor of Reuben Reuben, who was back in the town where his grandfather had been a boy.

The drum dance in traditional Inuit clothing was incredible. The drummers kept a deep, dark rhythm that pounded at my soul. The chanting and the dancing mesmerized us. It went on for half an hour, but it felt like barely a couple of minutes had gone by.

Then, finally, we had a chance to spend time alone with Elizabeth.

In the school staff room, she handed Reuben and me each a piece of dried caribou. I began chewing.

Dried caribou is prepared very simply. Strips are cut off a freshly killed caribou and then placed on a frame of sticks until the sun and wind dries the meat. Chewing adds moisture. So you end up eating raw caribou. I didn't like it as much as, say, a chocolate bar. I passed on a second helping. Reuben did too.

"Cold out there," Elizabeth said. "Nearly enough to make tires square."

She wasn't joking. When it got really, really cold, tires froze square on the bottom.

"Nice to be inside," Reuben said.

"Tonight," she said, "you spend the night sleeping with my husband, Sam."

Reuben and I looked at each other. This didn't make sense.

"I thought you had something for me from my grandmother," Reuben said.

"First thing in the morning," she answered. "After you spend the night with Sam. He's in the igloo already. He made it this morning. He's waiting in it for you."

The igloo was outside of town, where Sam had made the circular dome from blocks of snow. He'd used a stone lamp and burned whale oil to melt the inside of the blocks slightly, then let them freeze. The ice was a great insulator.

The wind had picked up, and the temperature had dropped. We only had caribou skin for blankets, but the lamp, plus our body heat, made it warm enough inside that I started sweating.

Sam didn't say a word all night. He just grunted when we entered. Then he fell asleep. And passed a lot of gas that smelled suspiciously like raw caribou. And sounded like live caribou every time he farted.

Let me just say, not a lot of fresh air moves through an igloo.

I was glad when morning arrived.

"Your ancestors could live through the coldest of winters," Elizabeth said the next morning, back inside the school. We had an hour before our flight left for Colville Lake. Buddy and Godzilla were packing. "How ingenious they were with such limited resources. You have an amazing heritage, Reuben Reuben."

Reuben and I thought we had part of this figured out. In each new town, we weren't going to get information until we first learned a lesson about the traditional ways. The one I had just learned was never to sleep in an igloo with an old man who ate raw caribou unless you had a set of nose plugs. And ear plugs.

"I am beginning to understand that better," Reuben said. He sounded like he meant it. "But I still don't understand my grandfather's life."

"Mike Reuben was a skilled athlete," Elizabeth answered. "I'm seventy-two now, but I remember him as boy. He drew the attention of all the girls. Much like you must do now."

I coughed.

"He fought a man in the south," Reuben said. "I'm learning more and more about that. Can you tell me what was stolen from him?"

"No," Elizabeth said. "Perhaps you'll learn that in Colville Lake."

We were headed there next.

By now I wasn't shocked to learn that Grandma Nellie had already guessed where the tour would take us. But it still drove me crazy, wondering how she'd been able to predict it so accurately, at least a month before the pond-hockey tournament had been set up.

Elizabeth handed Reuben a sheet of paper with Grandma Nellie's handwriting on it. *Look for Russell. Ask him more questions about this Chase.*

"This is it?" Reuben said. "I slept in an igloo for this?"

"You slept in an igloo for the same reason we teach the children here how to drum dance," Elizabeth said. "So that none of you forget. If you forget, how will you teach your own children? If the children don't learn, our ways will be gone from the world."

Reuben bowed his head in respect. Although I wasn't Inuit, I was starting to understand too. These elders were the link to the past. Once they were gone, the past would be gone. Unless Reuben's generation became a new link to their heritage.

"And there is one other thing I'm to tell you," Elizabeth said. Her eyes gleamed with humor. "Your grandfather had a glass eye. His left eye. Perhaps if you journey far enough, you'll find out how he lost his eye. And how he became a hero."

chapter seventeen

The next day was a whirlwind.

The farther we traveled, the more puzzling the mystery became. Mike Reuben had journeyed to the foreign world of rich people in Vancouver and had later been charged with assaulting Reginald Willowby there. Back up north, the RCMP had gone to question Mike Reuben, but he'd fled Aklavik into a blizzard that killed him.

We knew Mike Reuben was respected by all the elders in the Mackenzie delta communities. And that he'd lost his left eye doing something heroic. That was it.

Not only did Reuben and I have this whirlwind of questions around us, but we were also in the middle of a whirlwind of travel. Instead of flying from Paulatuuq to Inuvik and then on to our destination, we took a shorter route almost directly south to Colville Lake. Back below the tree line.

Runway: 2,743 feet. Elevation: 804 feet above sea level. As usual, someone was waiting in a truck to drive us to the nearby community.

We were no longer among the Inuit and Inuvialuit, but among the Sahtu Dene.

Where, we discovered, Mike Reuben had also made a name for himself.

"Let me tell you something," Russell Kessler said. "You could tie one end of rope to Mike Reuben and the other end to a moose, and Mike Reuben would be able to drag the moose."

Russell Kessler was an elder. He was missing two fingers of his right hand. He said it happened because a bear trap had been smarter than he was. Then he grinned.

We sat near a window at the Colville Lake School, Reuben and I in our Matlock Construction coats. Godzilla was with Buddy again, going over the airplane to get ready for our next flight. The game here had been another win for us—on an outdoor rink—and we were glad to be sitting, not skating. Glad to be out of the cold too.

Fewer than one hundred and fifty people lived in Colville Lake. It was so difficult to reach that a can of Coke cost nearly five dollars. The view made it worthwhile though. The lake was below us. We could see the cabin that belonged to Bern Will Brown, one of the most famous men to travel the North. We could see the church that he'd help build—Our Lady of Snows. He had come to the North as a Roman Catholic priest, and he'd helped people build new communities, including Colville Lake. He was legendary for his ability to travel on foot in the coldest of weather. He was also an author and a famous painter. Some of his artwork was in the church.

"I wish I could have been there that day," Russell said. Big grin again. "The day that Mike Reuben lost his eye. The grizzly that cost him his eye didn't live long enough to tell other grizzlies about it, I can tell you that."

"He shot the grizzly?" Reuben asked.

"Mike Reuben didn't have a rifle nearby," Russell answered. "He was chopping wood. All he had was the ax in his hand when he heard someone screaming for help."

We leaned forward. "Who?" Reuben asked.

"The man whose life he saved," Russell said, "by killing the grizzly with that ax."

"Whose life did he save?" Reuben asked.

Russell pointed at Bern Will Brown's cabin.

"My grandfather saved Bern Will Brown?" Reuben said. His eyes were wide.

"No," Russell said, "your grandmother asked me to make sure that you saw Bern Will Brown's cabin. And to think about a man and his accomplishments. A man like that could have been a success anywhere in the world, but Bern Will Brown made the North his own."

Russell patted a book he had beside him. "If you want me to tell you how to find the answers, you have to promise to read this book."

He picked it up and showed Reuben: *Arctic Journal*.

"Bern Will Brown wrote this," Russell told Reuben. "Learn from the great man. Reading is one of the best ways to acquire knowledge."

"I promise," Reuben said. "Now tell me who my grandfather saved from the grizzly."

Russell smiled one more time. "Open the book."

Reuben opened *Arctic Journal*. A piece of paper fell out.

Go to the cHurch in Fort Good Hope. Ask for a man named Joseph Fink.

And yes, Fort Good Hope just happened to be the next community on our tour. Even from a distance, Grandma Nellie continued to mess with my mind.

chapter eighteen

Fort Good Hope. West of Colville Lake. South of Inuvik. North of Norman Wells. Runway: 3,000 feet. Elevation: 268 feet above sea level.

Fort Good Hope is on a peninsula between a creek and the east bank of the mighty Mackenzie River. I loved being among the trees again. Hopefully, here we'd find more answers than questions.

After the game and a 12–10 win, we didn't go to a school this time. Buddy stayed at the small airport terminal with only Godzilla and the posters on the walls to keep him company. Our driver took us past Chief T'Selehye School to the church.

But it wasn't just any church.

It was Our Lady of Good Hope, perched on a bluff overlooking the Mackenzie. It was a small single-story wooden church. Long, with white wood siding, it was nearly one hundred and fifty years old. Maybe in the south a church with that kind of history doesn't seem impressive. But in the North, where most communities didn't even have roads to the outside world, it was old. And dignified.

Reuben and I stepped out of the truck under a gray sky with no wind. The silence seemed magnified because of the graveyard beside the church. Somewhere out of sight, a raven croaked.

I knew about the church because I'd flown on charters here before. Reuben had not.

He gasped when we stepped inside. Nothing about the exterior of the church gave any hint of the brightly painted interior and the stained-glass windows. The ceiling was blue with yellow stars. There were angel figures on a mural that covered the front of the church.

And there was the hush of silence.

We weren't alone though. Someone sat near the front, head bowed, as if praying. Our footsteps alerted him.

A Dene man stood and walked toward us. He was barely older than us.

"Joseph Fink," he said. "Are you Reuben and Gear?"

We nodded and shook his hand.

"This is for you." He gave Reuben another note from Grandma Nellie. *Pass the test at the mUseum in Norman Wells.*

Yup. Norman Wells was our next stop. Aaaack! How had Grandma Nellie known back in November?

"About my grandfather," Reuben said. "You'll tell us who he saved when he fought a grizzly, right?"

Joseph frowned. "I don't know anything about that."

"You're sure?" Reuben said. "Grandma Nellie sent letters ahead. We've been learning more about him at every community."

"I know that he helped my grandparents," Joseph said. "When they were alive, they talked about him all the time. He spent two winters here. My grandfather had a broken leg. He couldn't tend to his trapline. So Mike did it for him."

"Nice guy," I said.

"I don't think you understand," Joseph said. "Do you have any idea how much distance a man needs to travel on snowshoes to cover a trapline? And the weather he faces? Mike Reuben went out in the worst weather the Arctic can put in front of a man. And he traveled double the distance the other trappers did, with his trapline and my grandfather's trapline. Mike Reuben didn't want thanks. He just knew my grandfather needed help. Without it, who knows what would have happened to our family."

Joseph shook Reuben's hand again. "I know I can't thank your grandfather. So I'm glad I had the chance to thank you."

chapter nineteen

Norman Wells was where the commercial jets stopped on the trip between Yellowknife and Edmonton to the south, and Inuvik to the north. Runway: 5,997 feet. Elevation: 241 feet above sea level. If you followed the Mackenzie River far enough downstream from Norman Wells, you'd reach Inuvik.

To the west, in a sky that had turned pale blue over the last few hours, was the outline of the Mackenzie Mountains. To the east were the great Barrenlands of the North.

The town was a narrow stretch along the riverbank, and Buddy was going to use the down time here to fuel up and get some routine maintenance done.

Reuben and I thought we were going to unravel Grandma Nellie's mystery a little further at the museum. But the woman behind the counter sent us to Mackenzie Mountain School first.

"And then the big bad wolf lost to Little Red Riding Hood because she had learned how to kung-fu fight from the nice big panda."

That's how Godzilla finished his story. The school had asked Reuben and Godzilla to read stories to the little kids. Reuben had gone first, and then Godzilla, who had just finished talking to all the kids in grades one, two and three, making it up as he went along.

They clapped and cheered. The librarian smiled.

"Thank you," she said when the little kids left. "You don't know how much that means to them."

Godzilla just gave her his big warm grin. He never said much, but somehow you always felt and enjoyed his presence. On the ice, you felt his presence too, but I doubt players on the opposite teams enjoyed it.

"No problem," Reuben said. He put on his Matlock Construction coat as he stood. "Was this part of all the stuff my grandmother has planned for me?"

"Grandmother?" the librarian said. "No, we knew you were in town for the Matlock pond-hockey tournament. Could you sign this?"

The librarian handed Reuben a copy of the *Inuvik Drum*, the weekly newspaper. It had a huge photo of Reuben in his Oil Kings jersey on the front page. "The kids think you're a hero. This means a lot to them. Good luck in the three-on-three."

Technically, I scored a goal in the first thirty seconds of the three-on-three game against the players in Norman Wells. But only because Reuben fired a puck at my butt.

I'd half won the opening face-off, managing to dribble the puck backward. Reuben had scooped it up, and with the deafening cheers of another full rink, he'd deked each of the three players on the ice. I'd moved up ice with him, with Godzilla trailing.

Reuben had circled the end boards twice, and like everyone in the building, including the Norman Wells players, I had no idea where he was going next. So I parked myself by the net.

Without warning, Reuben had snapped a shot from the corner, banking it off my butt into the net.

He skated up and high-fived me. Godzilla did the same.

"Lucky," I said.

"Lucky?" Godzilla said. "Like you think that was an accident?"

"What else?" I asked.

Reuben tapped a spot just to the side of the net. The Norman Wells players were already heading back up the ice for the next face-off.

"Right there," Reuben said.

He began skating too. Godzilla and I stayed with him.

"Right there what?"

"Win the draw again. Then take that spot. Bend over with your head to the goalie. And close your eyes."

"Because?"

"Because," he answered, "I want you to be famous on YouTube." This game, like all the others, was being filmed by kids with video cameras.

I shrugged and won the next draw.

Reuben did the same thing as before. Dangled the puck as he skated, deking the players like only Reuben Reuben could.

I skated to the spot he'd tapped with his stick. As he went back into the corner, I bent forward. I closed my eyes.

A second later, it felt like someone had whacked the top of my helmet with a hammer.

Reuben had hit me with the puck. The crowd roared. Godzilla tapped my butt in congratulations.

I didn't even have to look up. I knew I'd scored another goal.

Technically.

We won the game 11–8.

"Yes, I've got something for you," the woman at the museum said. "But first, you take a good look around. If you pass my test, then you get the package."

"Test?" Reuben said.

"That was in the letter that came with the package. You spend an hour looking around. If you fail the test, you spend another hour."

"Oy, oy, oy," Reuben said.

"Pardon me?"

"Inside joke," Reuben said.

The museum was called the Norman Wells Historical Centre. It was also an art gallery and gift shop. Driving through Norman Wells, it was impossible to miss. It faced the Mackenzie River. In front of the museum was a paddle wheeler.

As we began looking around, I wished I had lots of cash. There were amazing aboriginal crafts. Beautiful paintings of the North. Books. Gemstones. Again, I realized how incredible the northwest Arctic was.

"Check this out," Reuben said. He pointed at ancient snowmobiles. "Imagine trying to get anywhere on these?"

I thought of the old biplanes that pilots of a previous generation had trusted to get them through the extremes of the Arctic. "We have it pretty easy," I said.

We checked out fossils and glacial history. I spent a lot longer at the aviation part of the museum than Reuben did.

When we got back to the front, the lady said, "You were supposed to spend an hour."

Reuben cocked his head. "We didn't?"

"Actually," she said, "it was two hours."

That surprised me too. Time had flown.

"Question number one," she said. "What is the Canol Trail?"

Reuben grinned. "One of the most expensive roads in history."

"Go on," she said, smiling back.

Reuben said, "During World War Two, when it looked like Japan might attack oil supplies in Alaska, the US Army built a trail and a pipeline from Whitehorse in the Yukon through the Mackenzie Mountains to Norman Wells to protect the oil. When they decided they didn't need the road anymore, they stripped it bare and abandoned it."

"Not bad," she said. "Next question. What's the thing you love most about the North?"

"That's not in the museum," Reuben said.

"That's the question I'm supposed to ask before you get your package."

Reuben thought about this for a while. "Not the northern lights. Not the wide-open horizon, where all you can see is snow and blue sky. Not even hockey." He paused. "It's the people."

Without saying a word, she reached behind the counter and gave him a brown package, about the size of a big book.

In fact, that's what we discovered it was when Reuben unwrapped it. A book of art. With prints of paintings by someone named A.Y. Jackson.

"This is it?" Reuben asked.

He opened the book. A piece of paper fell out.

Go to Tulita. And spEak to an elder named Johnny.

chapter twenty

A book of art by a painter named A.Y. Jackson.

What kind of clue was that? All we really knew was that Mike Reuben had lost an eye fighting a grizzly bear with an ax, but we still didn't know who he'd saved. All we could do was keep flying.

Which I didn't mind at all.

Wheels were down in Tulita the next morning. Runway: 3,000 feet. Elevation: 332 feet above sea level. We'd won in

Norman Wells too. We were seven for seven. Winning four more games would mean another five thousand dollars toward my dream of a pilot's license.

We stepped out of the plane to a clear cold day. Light snow crystals blew through the trees. I zipped up my Matlock Construction coat, grateful for the warmth.

"A hockey clinic?" Reuben said to Johnny, an elder with a firm handshake and a gray straggly mustache. "Was that in my grandmother's letter?"

"Nope," he said, "but you're here anyway for the three-on-three game. If you could spend a half hour on the ice with the kids, they'd be happy. Maybe not as happy as when Bryan Trottier came through a year or two ago, but pretty close."

Bryan Trottier was a Hall of Fame hockey player with six Stanley Cup rings and a seventh as an assistant coach. He visited the North a lot.

Reuben ran the clinic before the three-on-three game. And I went through the art book. Again and again. It didn't give me any ideas.

I read the notes in Grandma Nellie's handwriting.

Go to Sachs Harbor. There is A guide. Named JimMy. Meet him at the school.

In Holman, look for an elder nAmed Sarah. She has Good stories.

In PaUlatuuQ, an elder named Elizabeth will tell you more.

Look for Russell. Ask him more questions about this Chase.

Go to the cHurch in Fort Good Hope. Ask for a man named Joseph Fink.

Pass the test at the mUseum in Norman Wells.

Go to Tulita. And spEak to an elder named Johnny.

The out-of-place capital letters jumped out at me. Maybe there was a message in there. I put the letters down in order.

A-M-A-G-U-Q-C-H-U-E. Amaguqchue?

I played around with the letters to see if they made any words. It gave me a headache, and I stopped trying after about fifteen minutes.

Maybe we needed more letters.

After the game—a 10–7 win for us—Reuben and I said we needed a few minutes before the flight. We went to Chief Albert Wright School a couple of blocks down the road. It had burned down a few years earlier and had been rebuilt.

The walk from the community rink was pleasant. The temperature was only minus ten. Tulita had plenty of trees to block us from the wind.

The name meant "where the waters meet," because it was at the junction of the Great Bear River and the Mackenzie. Unlike nearly all the other communities in the western Arctic that had no roads to the outside in the winter, people in Tulita could actually drive to Edmonton if they wanted. It took them about thirty hours, with the first part of the trip down the ice road.

At Chief Albert Wright School, where we'd been invited to meet the kids, Reuben signed more autographs. I did what I usually did: stayed invisible and watched. Johnny, the elder, waited too. Finally, when we had the library to ourselves, Johnny spoke.

"Reuben," he said, "your grandmother Nellie sent me a letter asking me to tell you the story about your grandfather Mike. It's not much. But I was at camp on the shore of the lake when a grizzly bear attacked one of the men from the south we were guiding. I was fishing. I heard screams for help. I grabbed my rifle and ran toward the screams. When I got there, your grandfather had already stepped between the grizzly and the man. I couldn't shoot without hitting your grandfather. When the grizzly attacked, Mike took a mighty swing with the ax. It hit the grizzly in the head, but it was too late. The grizzly was on him. One of its great paws lashed out and caught your grand-father in the face as he fell. I was finally able to shoot the grizzly."

"What lake?" Reuben asked. "Who did he protect?"

Johnny's answer was to give Reuben an old black-and-white photograph.

"This was the day that your grand-parents married," Johnny said. "If you look close, you can see me there. That was nearly sixty years ago. I wasn't even twenty then."

The photo showed a group of people, all in traditional clothing. In the photo, Johnny was a strong young man, his face lit by a big grin. No mustache.

The people stood at the edge of the land, with water stretching behind them and some cabins off to the side. I decided the water couldn't be the Arctic Ocean, because there were trees in the foreground, and the Arctic Ocean was north of the tree line. The only lakes this big were Great Bear Lake and Great Slave Lake. Deline, a commu-nity on Great Bear was the logical guess.

We'd heard nothing about Mike Reuben doing guide work as far south as Great Slave.

Besides, Grandma Nellie had been right all the other times about which community would be next on our tour. We were scheduled in Deline next, and I fully expected her to be right again, no matter how crazy it seemed that she could have known ahead of time.

"Great Bear Lake," I guessed, "and the community of Deline."

"Wrong," Johnny said, his grin a reminder of the young man in the photo.

Wrong?

"Not Deline," he said. "Fort Franklin."

He was right. But I was right too.

Fort Franklin was about seventy miles up the Great Bear River from Tulita, where the river began to flow out of the lake and down to the Mackenzie. The old name was Fort Franklin. Now it was Deline.

"Nellie's letter to me said you are supposed to go there next," Johnny said to

Reuben. "Take this wedding photograph. It belonged to your grandmother."

Johnny stood and dusted off his pants. But they weren't dusty. It told me that he'd spent a lot of years working in places where he did need to dust his pants. Some habits just don't quit.

"One last thing." Johnny handed Reuben a piece of paper. *In Deline, show the photograph to an elder named Martha at Ehtseo Ahya School.*

I looked closely for a capital letter that didn't belong. Nothing. Maybe the other capital letters had been mistakes made by an old woman with sloppy handwriting.

As Reuben and I walked out of Chief Albert Wright School, I said, "Oy, oy, oy."

"Oy, oy, oy what?" he asked.

"For a few minutes you sounded like your grandmother."

"When?" he demanded, indignant.

"When you were talking to the little kids, after the hockey clinic. Telling them to stay in school and read a lot of books."

Reuben clutched his chest with both hands and staggered like he was having a heart attack.

"Trust me," I said, "being like Grandma Nellie is not such a bad thing."

chapter twenty-one

An hour later, we touched down at Deline. Runway: 3,933 feet. Elevation: 703 feet above sea level. From the road in front of the Grey Goose Lodge, the horizon opened up to Great Bear Lake. It was the largest lake entirely within Canada, the seventh largest lake in the world, and in places it was nearly 1,500 feet deep. But barely 500 people lived around the entire lake. I pointed at the frozen lake.

"First recorded hockey game in Canadian history took place here."

"No way," Reuben said.

"Eighteen twenty-six."

"No way," he said. "The Sahtu didn't play hockey then."

"Didn't say it was the Sahtu," I said. "British soldiers."

"Look, I'm weak on history," Godzilla said, jumping in, "but you can't tell me there was a war up here."

"Nope." It was fun messing with both of them. "Franklin's second expedition, up the Mackenzie River valley. He and his men stayed at the site for the winter." I paused. "That's why it was called Fort Franklin. His next expedition didn't work out that great. He got lost looking for a passage through the Arctic Ocean. Bad beans might have done the damage."

"Beans? Did they gas each other to death?" Reuben laughed. "Put that in history books, and us guys would pay more attention."

Godzilla laughed too.

"Not beans. A new invention: canned food. The cans were made of lead. There's a theory that lead poisoning messed them up."

"Man," Godzilla said, "how do you know all this stuff?"

He shook his head and held up his hand to stop me before I could answer. "No, Gear, the bigger question is this: Why do you inflict this stuff on other people?"

I had no answer. Except a grin.

Martha met us at Ehtseo Ahya School before the three-on-three game. She was teaching elementary kids how to speak Hare, the language of the Sahtu. She wore traditional clothing, and she had a broad kind face. She didn't seem to mind at all that we were interrupting, especially when we showed her the wedding photo with Reuben's grandfather.

She clapped her hands and grinned. "I remember that day! It was a joyful day.

The entire community joined in celebration." Just as quickly, her smile faded. "And a week later, it was horrible. Your grandfather nearly died. Only one week after the wedding."

"Grizzly?" Reuben asked.

"Just down the shore from here," Martha said. "I didn't see, but my husband was among the men who helped carry your grandfather to the lake, where a floatplane flew him to the hospital in Yellowknife."

"Who was the man from the south?"

"A famous artist," I answered. "A.Y. Jackson."

Martha looked startled. "Yes."

She held the photo in her gnarled hands. She pointed at another man in the background. "There he is."

Reuben looked just as startled. "Man, you scare me," Reuben said to me. "I can't figure out if you're psychic, or psycho."

Instead of explaining, I opened the art book and handed it to Martha. Reuben looked over Godzilla's shoulder.

"Ever see something like this?" I asked Martha.

I pointed at a sketch. The title of the sketch was *Franklin, Great Bear Lake, 10 September 1951*. There were a bunch of other sketches and paintings of the area. That's what I'd been looking at while Reuben played hockey with the kids.

"Yes," Martha said, "that was the man. Very famous. Very nice. He'd show us his work at the end of each day."

Martha wasn't able to tell us anything else. She just had the sheet of paper that Reuben and I had learned to expect. This one didn't have any misplaced capital letters either.

Go to Fort Mac. Ask for Suzie.

chapter twenty-two

Fort McPherson. Runway: 3,500 feet. Elevation: 142 feet above sea level.

But we didn't land on the runway. Good thing, because we were in a car. After a win in Deline, we'd flown the charter from there to Inuvik late in the afternoon. In the morning, we'd borrowed a car from Philip Collins and headed south on the Dempster Highway. We had two games that day—one at Fort Mac, the next at Tsiigehtchic. Win both, and I'd be ahead five thousand dollars.

As I drove, Reuben and Godzilla had asked me to tell them what I knew about the highway. I'd been happy to have the chance to show off what I knew about the North. "The Dempster is the only year-round road in Canada to cross above the Arctic Circle," I said. "It's gravel. Two lanes. Nearly five hundred miles from Dawson City to Inuvik. If the weather in the winter is good, that's a minimum twenty-hour drive. Twice a year, though, Inuvik's cut off from the world by road. Once in the spring when the ice bridges break up, and once in the fall when the returning ice stops ferries from crossing the Peel River and the Arctic Red River.

"What's really cool—literally—is how engineers made sure the road wouldn't sink into the permafrost. The highway sits on top of a gravel pad anywhere from four to eight feet thick. Otherwise the permafrost below it would melt, and the highway would disappear."

As I finished speaking, I heard snoring. From both Reuben and Godzilla.

Jerks. They had only wanted me to bore them to sleep.

Fort Mac was mainly Gwich'in. Nearly eight hundred people lived there. And one of them made us tea when we arrived.

We stopped at Chief Julius School after our game, our ninth win in a row. Godzilla was with us for a change. We had told him about the letters from each community and all of the stories. We showed him the letters too and asked if he could make sense of *Amaguqchue*. So now he was curious too.

It was a bright day, and the white of the school's exterior bounced sunlight across the snow. The principal there told us where Suzie lived. Her small home was set among the others on the east bank of the Peel River. Moose tracks covered her front yard. Inside, her curtains were wide-open and the home was filled with sunshine.

"First, drink," she said. Her hands shook a little as she poured from a pot. She filled her own cup. Added a few lumps of sugar. Sipped. And smiled.

The tea was so hot it took about fifteen minutes to empty our cups. Suzie used that time to show us photos of her grandchildren and to tell us stories about them. I wanted to hear a different story.

When Reuben finished his last sip of tea, he asked, "You knew my grandmother?"

"I lived in Aklavik as a young woman," Suzie said, "before I was married and moved here with my husband, God rest his soul. I hadn't heard from Nellie in a long time. I was happy to get her letter. And happy to hear that she would be sending her grandson to visit me."

"You knew about my grandfather," Reuben said. "That he was wanted by the RCMP. That he ran away and a blizzard hit."

"I did," Suzie said. "After getting the letter from your grandmother, I remembered how I wished he had defended himself in court instead of running. But sometimes that doesn't lead to justice."

She shook her head. "Hard to believe it began twenty-five years earlier when Mike Reuben lost his eye to a grizzly."

Reuben and I leaned closer. Were we finally going to learn everything about the mystery?

"When your grandfather was in the hospital recovering from the attack," Suzie said, "the doctors said he wouldn't make it. But Mike Reuben proved them wrong. He was a strong, strong man. It took him five weeks, but finally he was ready to leave the hospital. That's when he returned to Aklavik with Nellie. This was only a couple of years before the government decided it flooded too much and started talking about moving Aklavik across the delta."

Suzie closed her eyes in memory. "Many were the days that your grandmother and I would sit and have tea. Just like this. It did not seem like she was troubled for money, although Mike Reuben was still too weak to work. One day I asked her about it, and she said that a man from the south had sent them money because it was his fault Mike got attacked by the grizzly."

"Yes?" Reuben said. "Anything else?"

Suzie shook her head. "About a month after she told me that, I moved away from Aklavik. If anything happened after that, I'm not the one who can tell you."

I felt myself slump in my chair.

It was easy enough to guess that the man from the south was a famous painter named A.Y. Jackson. He was grateful that Mike Reuben had stepped in front of a grizzly to save his life, so he sent them money to help out. But there had to be more than that.

There was.

"Talk to this person," Suzie said. "He lived in Aklavik at the same time."

Suzie handed Reuben a note. No misplaced capitals to help me solve what may or may not have been a riddle.

Earl is the father of one of the teachers in Tsiigehtchic. Let him tell you what was stolen from our cabin.

Tsiigehtchic. Our last stop on the tour. Exactly as Grandma Nellie had known.

chapter twenty-three

Tsiigehtchic. Pronounced: sig-eh-chick. Population: under 200. Runway: zero feet.

Tsiigehtchic was one of the few communities in the North without an airport, and one of the few communities that was linked by road to the outside. Inuvik was only seventy miles away by the Dempster Highway except during spring break-up and fall freeze.

Tsiigehtchic was Gwich'in for "mouth of the iron river." It was on a bank overlooking the spot where the Arctic Red River fed into the Mackenzie. At this time of year, the bridge to cross the Mackenzie to Inuvik was ice. In the summer, there was a ferry. But in the fall, when the ice wasn't thick enough yet, and in the spring when the river was breaking up and the ferry couldn't operate, there was no way in and out of Tsiigehtchic except by helicopter. Good thing it was winter and the ice bridge was open, so we'd been able to drive. Reuben was barely getting over his fear of flying in airplanes; a helicopter would have made him lose all his hair from terror.

We drove past a small white Roman Catholic church on top of a bare, knobby hill that overlooked the river. We pulled up to Chief Paul Niditchie School and went inside. I carried the A.Y. Jackson book with me.

In the front hall was a huge mural with large letters that read:

*OUR TSIIGEHTCHIC ELDERS
KNOWLEDGE+EXPERIENCE=WISDOM*

Beneath this was a collection of photos of the community's elders. Reuben and I had just found the photo of Earl when a middle-aged man walked up to us. He noticed us pointing at Earl's photo.

"That's my father," he said with pride. The relationship was obvious. The man in the photo had piercing dark eyes and a furrow in his forehead. Just like the man giving us a quizzical look now.

"I'm Reuben Reuben," Reuben said. "We hope to talk to him about my grandmother and grandfather, Nellie and Mike Reuben."

The man nodded. "And I was hoping that you were Reuben. We've been expecting you. I'll call my father to come to the school. Maybe you can stop in the classrooms and talk to some of the kids until he gets here? You've become quite the hero to them."

In the library, there was a comfortable chair in the corner where Earl was waiting for us.

Reuben and I pulled up a pair of folding chairs and sat nearby. Earl didn't waste any time.

"Got to chop some wood today," Earl said. "Tell me what you want."

"Reuben would be glad to chop it for you," I said. "And I'll be happy to supervise."

Earl thought that was funny. He laughed loud and long.

"No," he finally said. "Prefer doing it myself. It's not even that I need a wood-burning stove. I just like the smell and the way it warms a house no matter how cold it gets outside. And I chop it myself because I don't want to get lazy. So tell me what you want."

"You knew my grandfather," Reuben said. "Mike."

"Great man. An honest man. Never let a friend down."

"Remember the summer that he lost his eye to a grizzly? When you were living in Aklavik?"

"Yup," Earl said.

I had been talking things over with Reuben on the drive from Fort Mac to Tsiigehtchic. We'd come up with only one thing that a rich man from the south might steal from Mike Reuben.

I handed the art book of A.Y. Jackson paintings to Earl.

"Would you mind looking through this?" I asked. "See if there's a painting you recognize."

Earl took his time. He'd scan a page and shake his head. With each new page he turned, our chances of being right about the stolen object seemed to disappear. Earl got through every page, then shut the book.

"Not one," he said. "Who is this man?"

"Alexander Young Jackson was a landscape painter, one of the famous Group of Seven," I said. "He made a couple of trips to the North in the forties and early fifties. He was the man that Mike Reuben saved from the grizzly bear. He died in 1974. Some of his paintings today are worth close to a million dollars."

Earl blinked. Then blinked again.

"That might explain something then," Earl said. He turned to Reuben. "In the fall, just a couple of months after your grandfather fought the grizzly, I walked into his cabin one day and saw a painting on the wall. It wasn't any of these, but it was the same style.

"It hung there for years and years," Earl said. "Then one winter I came to visit and it was gone. I asked Mike about it, and he said it disappeared the same day someone took the guest book they used for all the people he guided hunting and fishing."

"What summer?" I asked.

"I've never been one to pay attention to numbers," Earl said. "But I remember that was the year when the oil pipeline was opened in Alaska. After I heard from Martha that you were on the way, I asked my son to look it up on the Internet. The pipeline opened in 1977."

"Do you have a letter or something to give to me?" Reuben asked. "From my grandmother?"

"No," Earl said.

This was the end of our journey? It didn't make sense.

"Earl," I said. "One last question." I pulled a piece of paper out of my pocket. "Does this mean anything to you?" I asked. I showed him the letters I'd written on the paper: *AMAGUQCHUE*.

He frowned as he studied it. "Get me a pencil."

I found one on the library desk.

"If you put a space here," he said, "it becomes two words in Inuvialuktun." He drew a line where the space belonged.

AMAGUQ/CHUE.

"*Amaguq chue*," he said. "The first word means 'underfoot.' The second word means 'beaver.' It would mean something like a child playing under the feet of a beaver, the way a child gets underfoot among adults."

And that was all he could tell us.

chapter twenty-four

"Boys!" Danny Matlock bellowed. That was how he spoke most of the time—at full volume. His voice filled a room. So did his presence. The room he was filling now was our dressing room, just before our final game in Tsiigehtchic.

"Figured you'd get here undefeated," he said. "Good for you. Let's make the last game interesting. If you win, each of you gets a big-screen television. Got it?"

Reuben and Godzilla and I all nodded at each other. And grinned.

Disaster struck with a minute remaining in the last five-minute period.

We were a goal down. That wasn't the problem. It was me. Stepping on the blade of the stick of a Tsiigehtchic player. Falling into the boards. Sticking my hand out to save myself from a face plant.

And feeling a horrible snap as the fingers of my left hand bent backward.

No one heard me scream. The fans were yelling too loud.

I managed to get to my knees. The play had continued. Probably didn't look like anything worse than a routine fall to anyone. I grabbed the stick with my right hand and tried to get back into the action.

The puck was coming my way. Reuben had just fired it past the Tsiigehtchic player whose stick I'd stepped on.

What could I do?

One-handed, I tried to control my stick. The puck bounced off it. But no one was close, so I could stab at it again. I saw Godzilla open just ahead of me. I poked the puck, and it barely reached him. He spun with it and fired a pass onto Reuben's blade.

No hesitation. Reuben snapped a shot over the goalie's shoulders.

Tie game!

But there were only thirty seconds left on the clock and no way I'd be able to use my hand.

"Ref," I said. "Can you give me an injury time-out?"

He nodded. The clock stopped.

I gritted my teeth and skated over to Reuben and Godzilla to deliver the bad news. I'd never felt pain like this.

"Broken?" Reuben said. "You sure?"

"If I pull my fingers out of the hockey glove," I said, "there's no way they're going back in again."

Godzilla tapped my shin pads with his stick. "No problem, bud. Reuben and I will finish the game."

Except it was a problem. The Tsiigehtchic team was good. With two players, that meant one to take the draw and the other to get the puck. Reuben and Godzilla were the best players on the ice. If they had possession of the puck, chances were they'd find a way to score, even with the two of them against three.

But this would work only if the draw was perfect and the two of them got immediate possession. Otherwise the Tsiigehtchic players would pounce on it. And three against two was tough to defend against.

"Get some stick tape from the bench," I said. Danny Matlock was standing there as honorary coach. "Let's see what we can do."

"Tape," Reuben repeated.

"I want a big-screen television," I said, teeth still gritted. And I wanted ten thousand dollars from Matlock Construction instead of five for my pilot training.

The only good thing was that I'd broken the fingers on my left hand. Without taking my hand out of the hockey glove, I could only guess how many. The pain was blended together. Two fingers, maybe three.

But the left hand was the top hand on my stick. To win a draw, I still had my right hand, lower down, to grip the stick and move it.

Reuben came back with the tape. I tried not to scream as I placed my left hockey glove on the top of the stick.

"Wrap it in place," I said to Reuben. "As tight as you can."

I kept my jaw clenched as he did it. Pain washed through me. When he was finished, the stick was secure.

"Let's rock and roll," I said.

I moved to the face-off circle and bent over. I curled my right hand over the shaft of the stick. It made it obvious that I was going to try to pull it back to the right, but there wasn't much choice.

Somehow, as the puck fell, I managed to time it perfectly. I knocked the puck back to Godzilla. Then my stick clashed against the stick of the opposing center. The pain was white heat going up my left arm.

But it motivated me to skate hard.

All that the Tsiigehtchic players could have guessed was some kind of injury, but not how bad. So I bluffed. I broke for open ice, yelling for a pass. It forced one of the three of them to stay with me.

That gave Godzilla the room he needed. He broke past the guy in front of him. Reuben was already a blur going past me.

He took the puck at full stride. Didn't try anything fancy. Just swept around the last Tsiigehtchic player, cut back in and fired a backhand through the goalie's legs as the buzzer sounded.

Victory!

It was a great ending to the tour.

At least it should have been. After the game, we discovered our jackets had been stolen. And, after Danny Matlock had left in a helicopter, we also discovered our car wouldn't start.

We had to stay the night in Tsiigehtchic.

Broken fingers, stolen jackets and a car that didn't work. It was all bearable because we'd won. I thought nothing could spoil our victory mood. But in Inuvik the next day, I discovered I was wrong.

Very wrong.

chapter twenty-five

"Your grandmother is unconscious," the doctor told Reuben. The doctor was a tall dark-haired woman with a sympathetic expression. "She slipped and fell on some ice outside her home. Her head landed on the steps."

This was not the homecoming that Reuben had expected. We'd managed to catch a ride into Inuvik, dropping Godzilla off at the airport. Lizzie had not been able to reach us by telephone, and as soon as we'd seen her at her house, she'd rushed us to the hospital. The aunt Reuben and Lizzie stayed with in Inuvik was in Yellowknife and would fly back as soon as she could.

That morning, neighbors had found Grandma Nellie on the steps, and a charter had made an emergency flight from Aklavik to Inuvik.

"All her vital signs are good," the doctor continued. "She has a strong heartbeat and is breathing on her own. She could come out of it at any time. I think you can hope for the best."

Reuben nodded. Lizzie held his hand.

"I understand she's your legal guardian," the doctor said.

"Yes," Reuben said, "but this is a small community. We won't be alone."

"That's not what I meant." When the doctor smiled, the smile reached her eyes. "Philip Collins left a message with me. He wants you to visit him right away."

"Sure," Reuben said. "Thanks."

She walked away. Before she was out of sight, Reuben said to me. "Gear. Don't leave yet. Come to the lawyer with us."

Lizzie nodded at me. She was fighting tears.

Like I was going to say no.

"Reuben, Lizzie." Philip Collins got up from behind his desk to shake their hands. "I'm so sorry to hear about your grandmother. The doctors tell me that she has a good chance of pulling through."

He waved us into some armchairs with stuffing that had worn down to nothing.

"Gear," Philip said, turning his head toward me, "Nellie spent a lot of time during our phone call describing you. She believes you are a remarkable young man."

For once, I didn't make a wisecrack. I hated the thought of Grandma Nellie not in her cabin, not making life miserable for me and Reuben. I missed it already.

"Phone call?" Reuben said.

"In October," Philip said. "I found my notes. October seventeenth, to be exact. I don't suppose she ever sent you a letter while you were in Edmonton?"

"No," Reuben said. "What kind of letter?"

I couldn't help but think about all the other letters that she sent in November to people in the communities we had just toured.

"That's just it," Philip answered. "That was the reason for her phone call in October. Nellie asked me to take care of a letter, so that if anything happened to her, I could pass the letter to you."

Philip frowned. "But I never did get the letter. I assumed I didn't quite understand the phone call and that maybe she'd sent it to you. And I never got around to calling her about it. I regret that now."

"Maybe she never wrote it," Reuben said.

"I suppose not," Philip said. He gave us a sad smile. "Let's just pray she comes out of her coma. Then we can ask her ourselves."

chapter twenty-six

Lizzie walked through the park toward me. The setting sun behind me shot beams of golden light into her smiling face and gleaming dark hair. She reached her hands toward me and leaned in to kiss me on the cheek. And without warning, a clanging fire alarm broke the peaceful silence and sent her running away from me as fast as she could.

That's when I realized I'd been dreaming. The phone was ringing right beside my bed.

I grabbed it with my good hand. The broken fingers on my other hand were taped in splints.

"Hello?" I croaked.

"Hello," a voice whispered, "it's Lizzie."

I checked my watch: 10:00 PM. I'd fallen asleep early, exhausted from the tour of the communities, more exhausted from worrying about Grandma Nellie.

"Funny," I said to Lizzie. I liked it that she was whispering. I thought of my dream. "I was just thinking about you."

Another voice broke in. "Hello?"

It was my mother. On the extension. Not the voice you wanted as a third party when the girl of your dreams was whispering to you on the phone.

"It's cool, Mom," I said. "It's for me. It's Lizzie."

"Hi, Lizzie," Mom said. "How is Grandma Nellie doing?"

"As well as we can expect," Lizzie whispered.

"Good to hear." Mom hung up.

"Lizzie," I said.

"Hey, I can't talk," she continued to whisper. "But meet me on the river. It's pretty important. It's about Grandma Nellie."

I was still half asleep: "River?"

"Where Navy Road goes onto the ice highway. Get there as fast as you can. I need your help."

A couple of hundred yards from the end of Navy Road, the engine of my old Toyota died. I tried starting it a few times, but nothing happened. I was only about a five-minute walk from the river, so I hopped out of the car. I was wearing a down-filled coat, gloves and a hat. And running shoes instead of boots. I'd been in a hurry to help Lizzie. This clothing was nothing like the heavy snow gear I took on charter flights, but it would be fine for half an hour outside. It was about minus twenty. A good temperature to wake me up.

I jogged slowly toward the river. I didn't want to run. Breathing at minus twenty can be painful if you suck the cold air in too deep. I passed a Caterpillar D9 bulldozer, a machine used to maintain the ice highway, sitting off the road.

Fifty jogging steps later, I reached the edge of the riverbank, where the road dipped down to the ice highway.

No sign of Lizzie.

I was worried, of course. Was she in trouble? What kind of help did she need?

I got closer to the river and almost yelled her name. But if she was in trouble, maybe it would be better to sneak up on her.

On the ice, I walked downstream on the east channel of the Mackenzie. Much farther upstream, the river was wide and deep, but here in the delta it had spread out in hundreds of channels. This channel was only about a hundred yards across, but I could imagine the dark water moving beneath the ice.

It was dark. And quiet. At the best of times, there wasn't much traffic on the highway. Now, nothing.

I saw a figure to my right, in the middle of the ice highway. I stepped onto the highway. It was smooth ice, cleared by heavy equipment, and about as wide as a regular highway. One difference was that heavy trucks couldn't go over about twenty-five miles an hour on it. If they did, they'd create a wave under the ice, and the truck would break through.

The figure ahead was a dark outline against the white of the snow. It didn't move.

"Lizzie?" I tried to speak quietly. "Lizzie?"

No answer.

I jogged closer.

"Lizzie?"

Still no answer.

It wasn't until I got close enough to touch the figure's shoulder that I realized it was a dummy. Literally. Like a dummy from a store window. This one was dressed in pants, a winter coat and a hat.

What was going on?

Suddenly, there were headlights and a low roar.

I looked behind me. It was the bulldozer, the Caterpillar D9 I had passed when I was jogging down the final stretch of Navy Road.

I stared.

It moved closer. And closer.

I waved. Surely the driver saw me.

The bulldozer didn't slow down.

When it was about ten steps away, I realized that whoever was driving it had no intention of slowing down. I took a couple of steps backward. Then a couple more. The blade of the bulldozer hit the dummy and broke it in half. The dummy's head rolled toward me.

That's when I began to run downstream on the Mackenzie ice highway, away from Inuvik.

With a bulldozer chasing me.

chapter twenty-seven

I felt, rather than heard, my shoes crunch on the ice. Hearing anything above the roar of the bulldozer was impossible.

I was square in the bulldozer's headlights. It threw my shadow ahead of me, a giant ungainly figure with arms churning. But I had to keep chasing my shadow or the bulldozer would run me down.

For about a minute, I actually managed to put a little distance between me and the bulldozer. Later, I would learn that a D9 has a top speed of just over seven miles an hour. Running hard, that meant a pace of a mile every eight minutes or so. Most teenagers can run that fast, just not for long.

I sucked down the icy air, but all too soon my lungs grew ragged from the cold. It felt like I was breathing in air from a red-hot furnace. My broken fingers throbbed, but that was the least of my worries.

The bulldozer stayed directly behind me. It wouldn't get tired. There was no way I could stay ahead of it, not with all the miles between me and where the Mackenzie entered the Arctic Ocean.

I turned off the scraped ice of the highway and plunged into deep snow, thinking maybe I could make it up the bank and escape. But within seconds, I realized that was a mistake. The heavy snow tried to pull me down, as if I were fighting mud.

I turned again and almost fell on the ice. I'd made it to my feet when I felt the blade jabbing against my heels. I shot forward again.

Who was doing this?

I couldn't answer that question. All I knew was, if I stopped, I'd be run over.

But after about a minute, with sweat drenching the inside of my jacket, I began to slow down. Strangely, the bulldozer slowed down too. I kept that pace, but all too soon I had to drop to a half-jog. All I wanted to do was lie down on the ice. But the headlights were too close, my shadow too large.

At the half jog, I expected the blade to bump me again. I imagined tumbling forward, dying beneath the blade or the huge steel tracks of the bulldozer.

But the driver slowed down too.

What was going on? If he wanted me dead, why not run me over? And if the driver didn't want me dead, why keep chasing me?

I thought of dodging to the side and letting the bulldozer swing past me. But the time for that was gone. I should have done it near the dummy, when it was only a couple of hundred yards back to the bank and Navy Road. Here, if I dodged the bulldozer, the driver had plenty of time to swing it around and chase me again. I'd probably already gone a mile, and exhaustion made worse by terror had drained me. There was no way I'd manage another mile back without getting run over.

Then a horrible answer to my questions hit me. Maybe he didn't want to run me over. If the driver wanted me dead, this was the perfect murder.

All he had to do was chase me farther and farther down the ice highway until I collapsed. I'd freeze to death. And when they found my frozen body, it would look like I'd gone for a walk and couldn't make it back. It would be like chasing someone so far out into the ocean that they couldn't swim back.

I tested out my theory. I slowed to a walk.

So did the bulldozer.

I turned my head. I could see nothing except for the bright headlights.

I stopped.

The bulldozer didn't.

Its giant blade lifted high enough that I couldn't climb over. It bumped me. Like a cat pushing a half-dead mouse to get it to run again.

I fell backward.

Now the blade dropped and began rolling me down the ice.

It was obvious what would happen. Whether I ran or whether the bulldozer kept pushing, I was going to freeze to death. Unless I headed back to Inuvik and forced the guy to run me over. So what would be better? Dying quickly beneath a bulldozer blade? Or slowly as the cold froze me?

I scrambled to my feet and began jogging again.

The bulldozer stayed close. Relentless. I couldn't think of a worse nightmare. Unless the machine suddenly fell through the ice, I was dead. But this ice was so thick that tankers drove down the river. And tankers only fell through when—

I felt like I'd been jabbed again, this time by an idea.

I thought of a tanker I'd once seen. The back of it had fallen through the ice, leaving the cab just barely above water.

I didn't run any faster, although I suddenly had energy again. I had to trick the person driving the bulldozer into thinking I was running in a blind panic.

A couple of hundred yards ahead, the river curved. When I reached it, I left the scraped ice of the highway and I cut to the inside of the curve—the shortest line. The snow was nearly hip-high and slowed me down, but I wasn't worried any longer that the bulldozer would run me over.

If the bulldozer stayed on the scraped ice, there was a chance I could cut sideways fast enough to make it to the bank. If not, there was still something else that might save me.

The driver must have realized I might get away. The bulldozer left the ice highway and followed me through the deep snow.

I pushed and pushed. I was near collapse, but if I had any hope at all, this was it. A current moved fastest on the inside of a curve. The truck that had gone through the ice had driven off the scraped ice in a whiteout and had gone onto the thinner ice above the faster flowing water.

Was the ice thinner here too?

Above the roar of the bulldozer, an unearthly shriek suddenly answered my question as a crack in the ice snapped wide-open. I felt it too, a vibration that gave me another burst of energy. I threw myself to the side and dashed as hard as I could back to the center of the river. Away from the thinner ice.

The headlights of the bulldozer followed me briefly as it turned. Then the bright lights tilted up and over me.

I heard another loud crack.

I turned again, just in time to see the bulldozer fall backward into the river. As water washed over the engine, it stalled.

Silence. Blessed silence.

Then a scream for help.

The driver!

chapter twenty-eight

What I wanted to do was let the water take him away, to let the current sweep him under the ice. To have him feel the same helplessness I'd felt.

But in that instant, I knew if I did, I'd hate myself for the rest of my life.

The bulldozer had settled halfway down, blade high above the ice. Showing its deadly power, the current gushed over the lower section of the D9. The headlights were still on. There was enough of a glow that I could see broken ice and dark water.

But I couldn't see the driver.

"Hey!" I shouted. "Hey!"

No answer.

I couldn't trust that the ice was solid enough to get much closer to the bulldozer. For all I knew, the weight of the bulldozer had sent thousands of fractures through the ice. My own weight might take me through at any second.

I crawled forward to distribute my weight on the ice. When I was as close as I dared, I yelled again.

Still no answer. Just the gurgling of the water.

I'd been too late. The water must have swept him away. I nearly threw up, thinking of him tumbling down the river, trapped under that ice.

Slowly, I backed up, with snow crumbling over me. When I felt I was safe, I stood.

I needed to keep moving.

I turned back to Inuvik. After surviving this, no matter how cold it was, there was no way I was going to quit jogging until I reached town again.

At the RCMP station, the two constables on duty didn't believe me at first.

"A bulldozer chased you?" the first one said. He was a big guy. Young, with short dark hair.

"It's in the water. A couple of miles downstream. Why would I lie about that if all it takes is a short drive to find out that it isn't there?"

"Maybe you're the one who put it in the water," the constable said. "You were on some kind of joyride, and it broke through the ice, and now you come up with a story about someone chasing you on it."

"Look," I said. I was no longer scared. I was angry. "You think if I had done that I'd come straight to the cops?"

Without any warning, I wanted to cry, thinking about the guy under the ice. I had to clench my jaw to control myself. "Go look. Or don't look. Your choice. It's too late for the guy driving it anyway."

Within thirty seconds, the first constable was in his cruiser and on the way, red and blue lights flashing.

I was so exhausted I wanted to fall into the corner.

"Any idea who would chase you with a bulldozer?" asked the remaining constable, standing behind the counter. She seemed concerned for me. I appreciated that.

"None," I said. I was leaning against the counter, dripping sweat, still fighting to get my breath back. I repeated my story. "I got a call from a friend. I went to the river. There was a dummy on the ice. I thought it was my friend, so I went up to it. Then the bulldozer started chasing me."

"It was a setup? Whoever was driving the bulldozer was waiting for you to go to the dummy?"

I coughed. It felt like I was hacking clots of blood from my lungs. "Can't think of anything else."

"Any guesses why?"

"None."

"Would your friend know? The one who called you to meet her there?"

I thought of the way the caller had whispered. "Now I'm not even sure it was Lizzie."

"What do you mean?" the cop said.

I wanted to smack myself. *Lizzie! Maybe she was in danger too.*

"Give me the phone," I said. "Please." I dialed Reuben Reuben's number. No answer.

"Not good," I said to the constable.

Thirty seconds later, she and I were in another cruiser, lights flashing.

chapter twenty-nine

Reuben and Lizzie lived in the Aurora College housing, in a place called the Blueberry Patch. All the townhomes were painted light blue.

It took less than a minute to make it there. Of course, in Inuvik, it doesn't take long to get anywhere. Especially in a police cruiser with the lights flashing.

This late, it was quiet except for a three-quarter-ton diesel truck with its engine idling nearby. We ignored the truck.

On cold nights, a lot of people let their trucks run. Especially shift workers or someone who might get called in to work on short notice.

We raced to the front door. The constable knocked.

No answer.

She knocked harder. Still no answer. It was dark inside, except for the kind of flickering light that comes from a television.

Lizzie and Reuben lived on the main floor. There was no way they could sleep through knocking that loud. If they weren't inside, where could they be this late at night?

I thought of the bulldozer. Had the driver tricked them the same way earlier? Were they somewhere out on the ice highway, freezing to death? Or already frozen?

I decided to look through the window of the room where Reuben slept. I went around to the side of the house while the cop headed to the back door. As I walked through the snow to his window, I noticed something strange. Like a black snake slithering beneath the house.

I picked it up.

It was a garden hose. The end of it was somewhere beneath the house. In Inuvik, homes aren't built on the ground. That would melt the permafrost, and the houses would sink. There was a crawl-space under most homes, blocked by lattice or plywood to keep animals from getting underneath. One end of the hose led under the house. I pulled it out.

Why was the hose under the house?

The hose was buried underneath the snow. I lifted it and it came up, like the mid section of a snake. Where was the other end?

I kept lifting and following, lifting and following. The hose was hidden under the snow all the way across the yard.

Then I understood.

I yanked the hose. But the connection at the other end didn't break loose. It had been duct-taped to the end of the truck's exhaust pipe!

I spun and ran back to the house. With my elbow, I smashed the bedroom window, spraying glass inward. I backed away, moved to the other bedroom window and did the same thing.

"Are you nuts?" the constable hissed at me, coming around the corner of the house.

"No, scared! Knock the door down!"

"What? If this is a hostage situation, you can't just—"

I was already racing past her toward the front door. I threw myself at it, turning my shoulder to take the impact. The door hinges snapped out of the door frame. Cold air followed me inside.

With my good hand, I snapped on a light switch. The television was on with the sound turned down. Lizzie and Reuben were on the couch, as if they were watching the television. But they looked like wax figures. Eyes closed. Motionless. Their faces were an unnatural bright red.

"Get them outside," I said. "Please! They need fresh air!"

The constable didn't stop to ask why. As I bent down and put Reuben over my shoulder, she was doing the same with Lizzie.

He was heavy, but I didn't notice. Fear pumped too much adrenaline into my system. I dumped Reuben on his back on the snow. I didn't care that he was only in blue jeans and a T-shirt. I put my head against his chest. I heard one of the most wonderful sounds in the world: a steady *thump-thump-thump*.

"Is Lizzie okay?" I shouted. "Is she alive?"

The constable nodded.

"What's the treatment for carbon-monoxide poisoning?" I asked.

"Oxygen. Administered by gas mask. But what makes you think—?"

I pointed at the diesel truck that was idling in the cold night air. "There's a garden hose attached to the exhaust pipe. The other end was under the house."

Yes. Under the house, where the carbon monoxide would rise because it was on heated air, and where it would find the tiniest of leaks and slowly fill the house. Another perfect murder. Nobody in Inuvik thought twice about an idling truck. The hose had been hidden under the snow. Let the truck run all night. Chase me down the ice highway. Come back here. Drive away just before dawn, taking the hose with you. Leave Reuben and Lizzie behind—dead.

With the truck gone, nobody would know where the carbon monoxide had come from. This would be ruled an accidental death. Just like the frozen person who had wandered too far downriver.

But why would someone want all three of us gone?

The constable looked from the truck to the house and back to the truck again.

She could see the hose trailing down into the snow. She grabbed her radio unit and called the hospital and told them to get oxygen tanks ready.

We didn't wait for an ambulance. We drove Reuben and Lizzie there ourselves.

Three minutes after we got to the hospital, both were breathing oxygen through masks.

Five minutes later, Reuben woke up. Another minute after that, Lizzie did too.

And, finally, it seemed like I could start breathing myself.

chapter thirty

"It was the most amazing luck ever," I said to Danny Matlock. "I got a call from Lizzie last night to meet me at the river. So I went straight to Reuben's house to get help. My car quit on the way there, so I ran the rest of the way. I knocked and they didn't answer. When I looked inside, I could see them on the couch. Turns out they had carbon-monoxide poisoning."

We were in Danny Matlock's office, just down the hallway from the office of

Philip Collins. Danny was looking at me and Reuben with a furrowed brow.

"We still haven't figured out where the carbon monoxide came from," Reuben said. "We're just glad to be alive."

If there ever was a good reason for lying, we hoped we had it now.

"Strange," Danny said. "I'm so glad you all are fine. But it sounds strange, a call from Lizzie for help. Did she make the call?"

"No," I answered, "that's the weird thing. And something else is weird. My car. Someone had poured water into my gas tank. That's why the engine quit. Just like what happened to the car that Philip Collins lent us to go to Tsiigehtchic."

Danny showed even more concern. "That is really, really strange. Any idea why someone would do this?"

Reuben nodded. "I think it's because of a rare painting. Might be worth as much as a million dollars."

Danny leaned forward and frowned. "A painting?"

"By A.Y. Jackson," Reuben said. "The painter. If this really is about a painting of his that the public has never seen, whoever owns it will be extremely rich."

Reuben looked at me and nodded.

"It's like this," I said. I told Danny what Reuben and I had learned on the tour in each community.

In 1951, a couple of weeks after his wedding, Mike Reuben had helped guide A.Y. Jackson on his final trip to the Great Bear Lake region. Armed with only an ax, Mike had stepped between A.Y. Jackson and a grizzly. In saving the artist's life, Mike Reuben had lost an eye and spent weeks recovering in the hospital. Later, back in Aklavik, he'd been unable to work, but A.Y. Jackson had sent money to help. And, a couple of months later, A.Y. Jackson had also sent the gift of a painting.

This painting had hung in Mike Reuben's cabin for over twenty-five years, until a rich hunter from the south named Reginald Willowby had seen it during a guided trip and recognized it as an A.Y. Jackson. Willowby had stolen it late in 1977 and taken it back to his mansion in Vancouver. He'd also taken the guest book, so his name wouldn't be found.

But Mike Reuben had Willowby's address from a receipt, and he flew to Vancouver to get the painting back. By then, A.Y. Jackson was no longer alive, so Mike Reuben couldn't even prove that such a valuable painting had been given to him by the famous artist. Reuben was a strong man and a great athlete, so he wrestled with Willowby and took the painting by force. He fled the house with the painting and got on the next flight to the North. It didn't take long until the RCMP in Aklavik were notified of the theft. They went to arrest Mike, but he ran away, unprepared for the blizzard that killed him.

I finished telling Danny the story, and I took a deep breath.

"If this is true," Danny said, "what happened to the painting after Mike Reuben got back from Vancouver with it?"

"He probably gave it to his wife, Reuben's Grandma Nellie," I said. "She would have hidden it. After all, how could she prove it was rightfully hers?"

Danny leaned forward. "So the painting is still up here somewhere? I mean, we can't ask Nellie; she's in a coma."

This time, both Reuben and I nodded.

"The painting must still be here," Reuben said. "If it's worth a million dollars, it would explain what happened last night. Maybe the person who tried killing us also attacked Grandma Nellie. Just to get and keep the painting."

"You're saying Grandma Nellie's fall wasn't an accident?"

"Maybe not," Reuben said.

"What's really strange," I said, "is how Grandma Nellie knew we'd be on the hockey tour and the exact order of the communities we would visit. She sent letters out to the communities in early November. Philip Collins said you got the idea for the tour in late November and you didn't plan the tour until December. How could she have known about the tour?"

"I agree," Danny said. "That's very strange."

"There's another reason that might make more sense though." I took another deep breath. "Maybe it happened the other way around."

"I don't understand," Danny said.

"Maybe after Grandma Nellie picked out each person in each town for us to visit," Reuben said, "someone found out about her plan and decided to set up a tour that followed the order she had chosen. That way they could use me to find out about the painting."

Danny became very still. "What are you suggesting?"

"What he's suggesting," I said, "is that Philip Collins got a letter from Grandma Nellie explaining that if anything happened to her, Reuben should go from community to community to search for the painting. And the tour was planned by someone who already knew about the letters she had sent."

If possible, Danny became even more still. He spoke in a low voice. "You want me to believe that Philip Collins planned the tour in such a way that Reuben would be able to figure out where the painting was?"

"Why not?" I said. "All you'd need to do is hear everything anyone said to Reuben during the tour."

"This is ridiculous," Danny said. "Not Philip Collins. And how could someone listen to what people said to Reuben?"

"It would be very easy to plant a voice-activated listening device," I said. "Then you could download the conversations later. I did a quick Google search and found dozens of places that sell those kinds of spy devices."

"You could hide them in a down-filled coat, for example," Reuben said. "Especially if the coats are ones that the players are supposed to have on or with them at all times. You know, with the Matlock Construction logo on the back?"

"This is ridiculous," Danny said, half rising. "You can't accuse Philip Collins of something like this."

"You're right," I said. "But we can accuse you. You're the one who showed up in Tsiigehtchic for the final game. When you left by helicopter, our coats were gone and our car wouldn't start. While we were stuck there overnight, you had plenty of time to get back to Inuvik, listen to the recordings from the spy devices in our coats and go to Aklavik on the ice highway. If you had gotten rid of us last night, no one would have suspected anything."

Danny stood up and thundered, "I will not tolerate this. Get out of my office!"

"Not so fast." This voice came from Sheila, the constable who had helped rescue Reuben and Lizzie the night before. Philip Collins followed her into Danny's office. "We found this at your house about ten minutes ago."

She held up an A.Y. Jackson painting.

chapter thirty-one

Big as he was, I expected Danny Matlock to
fold right there.

Instead, he gave the constable a puzzled
frown. "You needed a search warrant to
steal one of my paintings from my own
house?"

"It belonged to Grandma Nellie," I said.
"You know it, and I know it."

Danny gave me the kind of smile you
save for babbling little boys. "How can
you be such an idiot?"

"You tried running me over with a bull-dozer," I said. He hadn't fallen in the river at all. He'd run into the trees. Earlier in the day, the RCMP had found a set of foot-prints that weren't mine, leading away from the bulldozer. "You yelled for help like you were drowning. To fool me into thinking the driver of the bulldozer was dead, so no one would look for him."

"Ridiculous."

He was using that word a lot.

"You tried to poison Reuben and Lizzie with carbon monoxide last night. There was a stolen truck hooked up to put the exhaust under the house."

He frowned at the constable. "I hope the RCMP isn't going to make the mistake of listening to this boy. I'm sure any decent lawyer would destroy his theories in seconds. And I'd really feel bad, having to sue for slander or something else that might result from hasty action here."

Matlock looked at Philip Collins. "Right, Philip? In fact, I may just sue over an improper search warrant. You people actually broke into my house based on this?"

Philip Collins coughed. Like an apology. "Sorry, boys," he said to me and Reuben. "You know I have a lot of sympathy for you. But so far, you don't have much that will hold up in court. And if you talk about this in public, he could sue for slander. It was a stretch for the judge to allow a search warrant."

"What happened?" I asked Danny. I remembered the day we first met Danny Matlock. Some of his mail had ended up at Philip's office. It probably happened in reverse too. "Did Grandma Nellie's letter to Philip in early November end up on your desk instead? Maybe a letter explaining to Reuben what to do to track down the painting? Your office is just down the hallway. Mail gets misdelivered once in a while. Right, Philip?"

"Go away," Danny said. "All of you. Before I lose my temper."

"The painting isn't proof?" Reuben asked the constable. "You found it in Danny's house. It belonged to my grandfather."

"Do you have documents showing this?" Danny asked, smiling smugly. "If Mike Reuben had owned it, he would have said something to the police when they were going to arrest him for assaulting Willowby back in 1978."

"Come on," I said to the constable. "What we're saying makes sense. Matlock's the only one who could have found out about this painting."

"I demand my painting back," Danny said. "Plus a letter of apology from the RCMP."

As Danny reached for the painting, I saw a long, thick, shiny hair on it. Like one from a pelt.

The constable was about to hand it to Danny, when I stepped between them.

I said two words as I looked directly at Danny. "*Amaguq chue.*"

His eyes widened slightly. I had him!

I turned to the constable. "Don't let him touch the painting," I said. "DNA testing can prove the painting has been in Grandma Nellie's cabin all this time. Hidden in plain sight."

Amaguq chue. Inuvialuktun for *underfoot beaver*. I remembered the morning in Grandma Nellie's cabin when I asked her why she had never sold the beaver pelt on the wall. The big pelt, stretched out. And now I think I finally understood.

"Reuben," I asked, "you know how we discussed the notes that Grandma Nellie had sent to each community? And we talked about the capital letters in odd places. Remember in Tsiigehtchic when Earl told us what it meant?"

"Yes..."

"So if Danny had found a way to record our conversations, he would have heard that. Especially after what Earl told us."

"Gear," Reuben said, "I don't know where you're going with this."

"*Amaguq chue*," I explained out loud. "Earl told us it means 'underfoot beaver.' The painting was hanging on the wall in your grandmother's cabin. Beneath the feet of the beaver. It was hidden under the stretched pelt that had been hanging on her wall for years. Danny must have figured that out when he went to Aklavik and hit Grandma Nellie."

"You'll never prove it!" Danny shouted. "It's slander!"

I pointed at the painting that the constable held. "See the long shiny hair on it? It's from a beaver pelt. There are more than a few stuck to it. It shouldn't be difficult to match those hairs to the beaver pelt in Grandma Nellie's cabin. Even if Danny stole the beaver pelt along with the painting, there should be some hairs left behind on the cabin floor. If they match these hairs with a DNA test, we've got all the proof you need."

Behind me, Danny roared.

I half turned. I saw a blur of motion. Danny had a letter opener in his hand, bringing it up to stab me.

I was dead.

Until Reuben dove into him, slamming him into the desk. The big man crashed through it. Reuben brought up a fist to punch Danny, but Danny didn't move. Reuben didn't have to punch.

The constable knelt quickly and began to handcuff him.

"Did that feel good?" I asked Reuben. This was the man who had bashed his grandmother.

He grinned. "Better than you can imagine."

chapter thirty-two

With my good hand, I handed Grandma Nellie a box of popcorn. My other hand still had broken fingers in splints. It was a month later. We were in the Rexall Place in Edmonton. The Oil Kings were tied 5–5 against the Kamloops Blazers. Overtime was about to begin.

"Popcorn to half-full," she said, scowling at me, "then butter, then popcorn to the top and more butter, right?"

I knew she was only pretending to be grumpy. Things had changed since Reuben had learned his family history. She had no secrets and was proud that he was proud of the North. The south wasn't a threat to her anymore, and she'd been delighted when Reuben and I offered to bring her to Edmonton to see him play.

"I got the popcorn just as you ordered," I said. "You sure are a lot of work."

"I'm worth it," Grandma Nellie said. "Don't you ever forget that, *Tullaaq Nookaa*."

Tullaaq Nookaa. She'd been calling me that ever since waking from her coma and learning about the night that Danny tried to get rid of all of us.

I was proud to have an Inuit name. She had told us that the reason she'd wanted Reuben to go from community to community was to learn more about his heritage and to have pride in it. Along the way, though, I'd learned an entire new respect for the North and the people who had settled it generations and generations before any modern conveniences.

Grandma Nellie had also confirmed what we'd suspected. After Reuben had been given a chance to go south to play for the Oil Kings, she'd sent a letter to Philip Collins to give to Reuben if anything ever happened to her. In the letter, she'd explained that she had a painting of great value and how Reuben would learn where it was by going on a tour of the western Arctic. At the same time, she'd sent ten other letters—one to each community—so that when Reuben arrived, he'd get the story piece by piece. The real reason was to send him all across the Arctic to appreciate his heritage.

"Explain to me about overtime," Grandma Nellie said.

The music was loud, and the crowd was getting into the spirit. Nellie was slapping her knees with her hands in time to the beat.

"First goal wins," I said. "If no one scores, then there's a shoot-out."

She grinned wide. "They better put Reuben in the shoot-out."

He'd already scored two goals and had three assists.

The referee made it to the face-off circle at center ice. He blew the whistle.

"Don't tell me you're proud of Reuben's hockey," I said in mock horror. "It's going to keep him in the south."

The painting had been estimated at a value of $800,000. Grandma Nellie was going to sell the painting and invest the money, putting aside enough to pay for whatever part of Reuben's education wasn't covered by the Oil Kings. I'd be at university too. Grandma Nellie was helping me as well.

"I can die in peace," she said. "Now I know the North is a part of him and he'll go back when he's finished with the south."

She patted my knee, a big smile across her old face. "And much thanks to you, *Tullaaq Nookaa*."

"It was nothing, really. Saving lives, solving mysteries. I do it all the time."

"That attitude is exactly why I call you *Tullaaq Nookaa*."

I puffed my chest in pride, even though the RCMP had done most of the work that confirmed our suspicions about Danny. They'd found the down-filled coats with the fabric ripped, as if something had been pulled out of them. They'd found charges on Matlock's credit card for listening devices that would fit in the coats. On his computer, they'd found e-mails that he'd sent out with photos of the A.Y. Jackson painting, offering to sell it. They learned his business was in trouble and he was desperate for money. And the biggest piece of evidence was that they'd found his fingerprints on the duct tape around the exhaust pipe of the stolen truck he'd used to pump carbon monoxide into Reuben and Lizzie's townhouse. That's when Danny had finally confessed that he'd learned about the painting when Grandma

Nellie's letter to Philip had landed on his desk by accident.

"What exactly does *tullaaq nookaa* mean?" I asked. I'd been wondering ever since she called me that. "Legend of the North? Wise man? Bright glory of the sky? Great hero?"

She patted my knee again. "If Reuben scores, I'll tell you. Otherwise, it's another mystery for you."

Godzilla skated into the face-off circle to square off against the Blazers' center.

The puck dropped, and Godzilla rammed his shoulder forward and fought for it. He managed to hold off the Blazers' center and kick it back to the Oil Kings' left defenseman, who fired it over to the right defenseman.

Reuben was cutting across the middle. He was briefly open, and the pass came a split second later.

The Blazers' center had broken loose, and he scrambled to catch Reuben.

But Reuben was at full speed, on a line to where the Blazers' blue line ran into the boards. Their defenseman was forced to shift with him. Then, incredibly, Reuben wheeled so hard that a spray of ice left his skates and flew into the defenseman's face.

Godzilla had burst forward as well. Just like that, two-on-one!

Reuben feathered a pass to Godzilla, who banged it right back to him. Reuben went wide, then backhanded it back to Godzilla, who fired a snap shot that the goalie managed to knock down with his blocker.

Reuben had been racing to the net. The rebound spun past him, barely within reach. Reuben managed to snag it, but his momentum had taken him too far past the net to knock it in with a wrist shot. He spun backward, and as he was falling away, flicked it on his backhand, just over the sprawling goalie.

Fifteen seconds into overtime—goal!

The crowd's roar lasted a full minute.

People around us began to file out of the stands. I stayed where I was with Grandma Nellie, who was happy to keep eating her popcorn. I knew exactly what I was going to say as soon as it got quiet.

"You owe me," I said to Grandma Nellie. "*Tullaaq Nookaa*. What's it mean?"

"A much-loved baby with poopy pants," she said. "Now find me something to drink. All this popcorn is making me thirsty."

Author's Note

While the characters in *Oil King Courage* are fictional, I've tried to make as many details of the story as accurate as possible, and I hope it gives you a sense of how amazing it is to travel among the people, the heritage and the landscape of the western Arctic. If you want to learn more, please go to: www.coolreading.com/visitthenorth.

A.Y. Jackson, one of Canada's most famous artists, did tour the North as described. The grizzly bear attack and the missing painting, however, resulted from daydreaming, one of the things I enjoy most about reading or writing a story. While Jackson's paintings are now as valuable as described in the book, I made up the story about Mike Reuben.

Acknowledgments

I'm fortunate to have wonderful memories of each of the communities in this story. This is only possible because of the commitment and generous sponsorship of Schlumberger Canada Ltd. to the *Literacy For Life* program. It has allowed me to tour the North with one of hockey's greatest legends, Hall of Famer Bryan Trottier, and he and I have shared our love of hockey and books throughout these great communities. (Check out www.bryantrottier.com for some amazing hockey highlights.)

Thank you then, first to Schlumberger Canada, and to the people and teachers and students in each community who made me feel so welcome.

Thank you, Bryan. It was an honor to spend time on the ice with you during the clinics and games hosted by each community.

Thanks, Paul Kruse and Al Conroy, for sharing your NHL expertise on the tours. It was an honor touring with you too.

Thanks, John McMullen, for your dedication to *Literacy For Life* and for the many ways you make the tours unique.

Thanks, Sarah Harvey, for your deft touch and encouragement and great editorial advice throughout each new draft of the story.